To Brum.

with out
I would only have been in a little pain.

Hope you enjoy

THE QUEST FOR THE TAVERN THAT GIVES CREDIT

THE QUEST FOR THE TAVERN THAT GIVES CREDIT

Richard Burns

The Book Guild Ltd
Sussex, England

First published in Great Britain in 2004 by
The Book Guild Ltd
25 High Street
Lewes, East Sussex
BN7 2LU

Copyright © Richard Burns 2004

The right of Richard Burns to be identified as the author of
this work has been asserted by him in accordance with the
Copyright, Designs and Patents Act 1988.

All rights reserved. No part of this publication may be
reproduced, transmitted, or stored in a retrieval system, in any form
or by any means, without permission in writing from the publisher,
nor be otherwise circulated in any form of binding
or cover other than that in which it is published and without a
similar condition being imposed on the subsequent purchaser.

All characters in this publication are fictitious and any resemblance to
real people, alive or dead, is purely coincidental.

Typesetting in Times by
Keyboard Services, Luton, Bedfordshire

Printed in Great Britain by
CPI Bath

A catalogue record for this book is available from
The British Library

ISBN 1 85776 821 3

CONTENTS

Foreword		vii
1	The Beginning	1
2	The Wizard	8
3	Cow-astrophic	12
4	Troll-ble Afoot	19
5	Lud	25
6	This could be Orc-ward	33
7	The Dragon	38
8	Brownie Trousers	49
9	The Curse	54
10	The Witch	62
11	Geraldine	74
Epilogue		84

FOREWORD

(The bit before the bit at the beginning)

Allow me to introduce myself to you good people. My name is ... er ... well ... I think my name is ... you know, it's on the tip of my tongue. Anyway, you must know me, tell me you know me – I can't remember who I am. Never mind, we'll get back to that a little later on. I live at number 1, Key Towers, in the small village of Crappy-Upon-Dung, in the land that was once called Oggle. I know this because it's engraved on my keys. It's a nice quiet village, where I work as the village drunk, having taken over from the previous incumbent a few years ago now, when he accidentally managed to cut his own head off while shaving. As for me, well, I've got pretty good at being a drunk, even if I do have to say so myself. It's not all beer and skittles being a drunk, I can tell you ... even if that's only because I don't know how to play skittles. No, my biggest problem was that the village boasted only one small tavern, 'The Cow Spillage', and no easy wenches; or at least no easy wenches that would look sideways at me. So even for a drunk life in the village was about as exciting as watching paint dry. That's just one of the reasons I wanted to leave, but I never really seemed to get the chance, that is until now ... or at least in a few pages' time, anyway.

1

The Beginning

It all began one beautiful Saturday afternoon. The bright sun shone down clear and bright, casting deepening shadows around the small village. Now, you might be wondering how I knew this, considering I was lying flat on my back outside the tavern, but I'm just setting the scene for you. So there I was lying on the grass enjoying the warmth of the afternoon sun on my face when the tavern door flew open with a bang delivering Meg, the landlord's wife, into the sunshine. Meg was a nice enough girl: big tits, brain the size of a small peanut, her perfume an intoxicating mix of sheep-dip and stale ale. She and her husband had run the Spillage for longer than I could remember, so at least from last Thursday. What was on her tiny mind today was the small matter of my rather large bar bill. Now when I say rather large, what I really mean is –
'Holy shit! I spent how much?'
Still, I reasoned, it was my professional duty as village drunk to run up a large bar bill, and the fact that I now owed her more than the cost of a nice castle in the country just showed how well I was doing my job. For some reason she didn't buy that line of reasoning. So, after sitting through about ten minutes of the worst tongue-lashing I had ever had outside of a brothel, I made up what was left of my mind that it was high time to start drinking at

another tavern: one that would give me credit, one that had peanuts on the bar, and one that had a pretty barmaid for a change. As soon as I could find my legs I'd be off.

Suddenly, a dark, menacing shadow loomed over me, obscuring the sun; that is, as menacing a shadow as a small drunken dwarf can cast. As the small walking smell that was Knobby slumped down on the grass next to me, I made the mistake of asking him how he was.

'Bloody awful!' he slurred. 'You know there's not one wench in this bleeding village that will even talk to me now!'

'That's because you've been out with most of them!' I smiled.

'And I still can't get any!'

'Yes ... but there's a very simple reason for that.'

'What?'

'You're an ugly bastard!'

Now I should explain a little about my friend Knobby, so you don't think he's just a foul-smelling, sarcastic, ugly dwarf. The fact is, he is a foul-smelling, sarcastic, ugly dwarf but there is a little more to him than that; not a lot, I'll grant you, but a little bit. You see, Knobby had been a circus dwarf as a boy, travelling from village to village with his family. The family's speciality was the shot-put. People would travel from miles around to take their turn in hurling the young Knobby into the air, but as the years passed and his belly grew, he grew too large to be hurled through the air, and it came to pass that one cold November morning his parents sold him for two sheep, one chicken and a bag of pork scratchings.

For a while we just sat there enjoying the gentle sun on our faces and the ale, trying to remember where and who we were. My memory seems to get a bit hazy after the tenth mug.

Suddenly, Knobby came out with an idea that sounded

vaguely familiar, and was to change our lives for ever, or at least for the rest of this book.

'I've been thinking...'

'I thought the doctor warned you about that.'

'You know what we should do, we should move to another village.'

'What, one you might get lucky in you mean?'

'And one you might get credit in. I hear she's cut you off.' He gestured towards the tavern.

There was a long pause while I mulled the idea over and then, because I'd forgotten what we were talking about, I agreed. Then I added, 'But only as far as the next tavern girl, right?'

Knobby having a few coins left, we ended up staying outside the tavern for just a few more drinks, and dusk was beginning to fall when Knobby said:

'What about old Big-Ears?' Big-Ears was Knobby's pet name for Boglith, the village's henpecked elf. The elf was a close friend of ours – whenever we could get past his wife, of course.

'No, you know he won't want to come, he's married.'

'I'm not too sure about that. You know he's been looking for any reason to get away from that tongue of hers for years now, not to mention that right cross!'

'I know, four hundred years of a nagging wife is enough to send anyone round the bend.'

'Or round the pub!'

'All right then, let's go and ask the morbid little sod. But you just know what he's going to say,' I said, getting shakily to my feet, and off we both wobbled. Sometime later, when we managed to crawl out of the very large puddle we seemed to have fallen in, we decided it would be best to go see him in the morning, or when we woke up, at any rate. So it was back to Knobby's hut for a few mugs of his home-brew, always a really bad idea.

The next morning I woke up at home, with a small chicken and two bras in bed with me, Knobby's brew had struck again. By the time I had recovered from my hangover it was way past sunrise. Finding Knobby still in bed, alone as always, the two of us went in search of the elf. It didn't take us too long to find him. He was at home being shouted at by his lovely wife, Silmare. We had to hide behind a water-barrel, as for some reason she didn't like the two of us very much, until she went out shopping, and it was safe for us to go in.

Boglith was small for a western elf, at just under six feet tall, with long, pearl-white hair. He would have cut quite a handsome figure, for an elf, if it hadn't been for his ears; they were by far the biggest any of us had ever seen. They seemed to have been stuck on his head as an afterthought, wobbling as he walked. He seemed to spend most of his sad life walking around with a look that cried, 'Please kill me, I'm married!' This morning he was walking around his house sporting a massive black eye and a very bent-looking nose, both presents from his ever-loving wife that morning. I had known Boglith for about four or five years now, and he had been married for well over four hundred years before that. Yes, Boglith really did want to die. The only small joy the elf had in his life he got the same way as every other married man has through the ages, by annoying his wife. Silmare was the kind of woman who could curdle milk with one look. Not so much evil, but grade A, mother-in-law material, if you know what I mean.

'So, how's it going, Big-Ears?' Knobby laughed, with a slap that sent the poor elf halfway across the floor.

'I suppose I'm OK, if you like that sort of thing,' was his weary reply.

'How's the wife?' I asked, knowing the answer before I opened my mouth.

'Angry ... as always,' he replied, with a long sigh.

'Sorry, mate,' I said with feeling.

'Look ... Knobby and I were thinking of going away for a little while, and thought you might like to come.'

'Where were you thinking of going?'

'Oh, just on to the next village girl or two,' I answered, pulling up a stool. 'You fancy coming with us, then?'

The colour started to flow back into Boglith's face. He was starting to look more elvish and less like a slap with a wet fish. I wasn't sure, but I thought I saw the beginning of a smile on his lips.

'How long you think you'll be gone?' he asked, the warmth returning to his voice.

'Hadn't thought about it much ... about a month or so.'

'If we come back!' laughed Knobby.

'You couldn't make it nearer two months, could you? That way I'll miss Silmare's birthday,' he said with a small smile.

'You're on,' I laughed.

With that, it was straight back to Knobby's hut to celebrate our adventure in style: more dwarven home-brew. Now, I feel I should explain a little about dwarven home-brew, and all dwarven ale in general. Through all the world's many lands, nothing can compare with the truly awful taste of dwarven ale. It's a little like sucking on a rock troll's arse, but the effects are far worse, and no one can really say what they will be, as they vary from race to race, and person to person. You never know what you're going to get until you finish that first mugful, and by then it's too late to do anything. If you're lucky it will just turn your brains to mush and your native language to gibberish, but if you're unlucky, it can have far more sinister and sometimes deadly repercussions. One minute you may seem perfectly fine, the next you will launch into the dwarven drinking song. More than one unlucky traveller has been slain for sitting in a crowded tavern singing, 'Gold, gold, gold...'

at the top of his voice. By the grace of the gods, so far I had been spared that awful fate; but believe me, nothing can take the dreadful taste away.

The next day dawned bright and clear. The birds were singing, the gods were in heaven, there wasn't a cloud in the sky, a gorgeous summer's day; the last bloody thing you want when you've got a hangover. It was more than a little later when I managed to dig myself out of the large ditch I had decided to sleep in. After rushing home to change, as I seemed to be wearing a little pink and white party dress, I went to find the others. Knobby I found face down under a wagon, hugging a very surprised and worried-looking sheep. When I finally managed to wake him up, he let his new friend go and together we went in search of Boglith. As the pair of us approached his house, we were more than a little amazed to find him flying out of the bedroom window.

'So, I'll be off then, my love,' he cried as he flew through the air head first.

We pulled him gingerly out of the large pile of dung he had landed in, and it was back to Knobby's hut to plan our adventure and, of course, wash the elf. After a few more mugs of Knobby's home-brew, and no planning at all, we were off.

It couldn't have been more than an hour or so before the three of us trudged back into the village for supplies. Take it from me, there is no point in going on any sort of adventure without a good supply of wine and ale, not to mention a large pack of aspirin. Now, all geared up, we were ready for our big adventure.

We were about two or three hours down the trail, dusk was beginning to fall, and as none of us seemed too comfortable in the deepening darkness, we decided it was about time to make camp for the night. Now, this proved to be our first of many problems, as not one of us had the slightest idea how to light a fire. So, with nothing else to do, we started on the wine and just fell asleep where we fell, conveniently on the ground, by the side of the road.

I would like to say a few words about the inadvisability of waking in the morning with your head on a rock and feet in a cow-pat. You'll be surprised to learn that I didn't see the funny side of doing just this, although the others did.

'Now you've really put your foot in it,' laughed Knobby.

'No shit,' smiled the elf.

The next small problem was breakfast. We discovered that not one of us had packed any food; lots of wine and ale, but no food. So we just drank a little more wine and started down the trail again once more.

Lunchtime came and went, with only a smallish glass of wine to keep our spirits up.

Dinner time came around with no hope of a meal, just more wine. As we drank the last of the wine by the roadside that night, we decided that if we couldn't find any food the next day, we'd just have to eat Knobby.

2

The Wizard

The next day dawned dull and overcast. A fine dew hung from every leaf and branch and the air was heavy with the promise of fresh rain. I was slowly roused from sleep by the rather unpleasant sensation of a black crow pecking at my head. There will be those that say this was a dark omen, but thanks to the crow, I was the first awake that morning and as I watched the others sleep, it occurred to me how great Knobby would look going round and round on a large spit, with an apple in his mouth. I was about to wake Boglith with this idea, when the most amazing smell of roasting meat floated over to me. After not eating for so long the smell of food was more inviting than any woman could be, unless of course she happened to have a plate of sandwiches with her. I wasn't sure what sort of meat it was, but I woke the others and together, our noses leading the way, we were off across the fields.

After making little or no progress for about ten minutes, up to our knees in cow-shit, we decided to use the path instead. It was about an hour or so later that we came across the tree, old and withered, a faded sign nailed to its blackened trunk, the letters too indistinct to read. By now I had to answer the call of nature, and had just started to water the tree, when a loud groan like metal bending filled the air, followed by one of the loudest bangs I've ever heard in my life. It seemed to echo in my ear, vibrating the very ground. I must have jumped about a foot in the air, spraying myself from head to toe. The smell of roasting meat grew incredibly strong and a strange, unearthly howl began, like a giant creature in pain, a high-pitched wail from somewhere high up. The sound was so unnerving that, being the true and brave heroes we all were, we ran away and hid. A flash of flame streaked across the sky, and where we had been standing not thirty seconds before, a small, very burnt-looking wizard smashed to the ground. At least, I assumed he had once been a wizard, since a large pointy hat on what was left of his head was something of a give-away. The smell of roasting was now overpowering.

'That'll hurt,' remarked Knobby.

'So that's where the smell's coming from,' I said.

'What do you think we should do with him?' Boglith asked, walking round and poking the smoking wizard with a stick.

'You could offer me a bloody drink for a start,' croaked the wizard.

'Bugger me, he's alive,' said Knobby.

'No thanks, you're not my type,' answered the wizard, getting shakily to his feet.

'Who, or what, the bloody hell are you?' demanded Boglith, reaching for his sword, or rather the place his sword should have been, if he hadn't forgotten to bring it.

'I am the all-powerful Gilbert, master of magic,' answered the wizard, planting both hands on his hips.

'If you're so bleeding all-powerful, how come you've just managed to blow yourself up?' asked Knobby.

'How do you know I blew myself up? Maybe I was in a mighty duel with an evil wizard.'

'Were you?' I asked.

'Was I what?' he answered, dusting the soot off his hat.

'Were you in a mighty duel with an evil wizard?'

'No, I blew myself up.'

'Some master of magic,' Knobby snorted.

'Well, I am only a true master with the ladies,' he replied with a smile.

'Bollocks!' snorted Knobby with real feeling, 'I've got over sixteen inches to spare, and I'm not a master with the ladies.'

'You see this ring?' interrupted the wizard, thrusting a blackened hand under Knobby's nose, on the middle finger of which sat a huge silver ring. 'It turns any woman into my sex slave. Anything I say, they do it.'

'You want to sell that?' asked Knobby.

'He hasn't had any for a while,' I whispered to Gilbert.

'So how does it work?' asked Knobby.

'Now ... well ... that's a small problem, you see. I bought it off this old guy, and I haven't got a clue how it works,' he answered, an embarrassed smile on his face.

'So basically it's a silver ring that does bog all – a lot like every other silver ring in the realm,' Knobby snarled.

'Basically ... yeah... So how about that drink, then?' Gilbert asked.

'We've run out of food and wine,' snapped Boglith.

'No problem. Come back to my place. There's food and wine back there,' Gilbert said, setting off across the fields.

An hour later we all sat in the burnt-out husk that was once Gilbert's house. Two of the four walls had strangely vanished and the gods only knew where the roof was. The rest of the house was burnt and blackened, but Gilbert still managed to find a bottle of wine and a roast, even if it did look suspiciously like a cat.

'Don't worry, it's chicken,' Gilbert assured me, handing me a leg. I couldn't help noticing that it was the fourth he'd given out. 'So, what are you lot up to, then?' he asked, sitting down with another bottle of wine.

'We're on a mighty quest,' said Knobby.

'What kind of quest?' Gilbert asked, taking a long pull on the bottle.

'To find a tavern that gives credit.'

'Ah ... a worthwhile quest, then.'

'Why don't you come along?' I asked.

'It's not like you've got a lot to stay here for,' put in Boglith.

'Why not? It might be fun, and it doesn't sound dangerous,' he answered.

From that moment on we were four. The four of us spent the night in what was left of Gilbert's house, as he managed to find even more wine. The next morning came and went, but we were all still out from the night before. Some time the following afternoon we finally woke up. After a breakfast of cold whatever and a few glasses of wine, the four of us were on our way again.

3

Cow-Astrophic

After three miserable days and nights of trudging along, up to our arses in mud and mire, our spirits lowering by the second, we came in sight of the next village. A small faded sign proclaimed this to be the village of Turd-by-the-River, and although large for the region, signs of neglect were apparent everywhere. The village church showed the greatest signs of decay, standing little more than a ruin in the centre of the village. The small one-room huts that lined every street and avenue had long since spilled out into the nearby fields.

Running through the centre of the village was a thick, black river, which gave the whole village a foul stench, one that almost rivalled Knobby after a Saturday night. The whole village was dark and depressing with only one small gleam of hope; the tavern was open. It wasn't long before the four of us were crowded round a small table, close to the hearth, the roaring fire warming our tired bones. As we sat there nursing one mug of ale between us, we all knew that this might be the end of our long quest and a very dry, sad end at that. The second we sloshed into the tavern, the barkeeper had taken one long, hard look at the four walking cow-pats in front of him and demanded to see the colour of our gold before he would pour us even a single drink. So now we sat around the small fire, with our one mug of ale and four straws, with nothing to look forward to but the long walk home.

'So that'll be our quest finished, then,' Knobby cursed.

'What, you mean back to the wife?' gulped Boglith, the colour draining from his face as he spoke.

'I don't see what choice we have,' I sighed.

'Come on, let's face it, no one...' But Gilbert never got the chance to finish his sentence, as the doors flew open with a crash, sending the occupants of the bar scurrying into the shadows. As we looked up the whole doorway seemed to be filled with a dark, menacing shadow.

'Shut that bloody door, it's freezing out there!' shouted Knobby, pulling his tattered cloak around his shoulders.

The menacing shadow entered, revealing one of the biggest sons of a bitch I had ever seen in my life. His brightly-polished armour and heavy iron helmet proclaimed him to be a knight; either that or a travelling salesman on the way to Boglith's house. The knight strode towards the bar, his gleaming armour clanging with every step. A large sword hung at his waist and over one broad shoulder a large bloodstained sack was slung. Swinging the sack onto the bar, the knight doffed his helmet shouting, 'Barman, ale!' Without a word the barman placed a huge mug of ale before him. Quaffing it in a single swallow, the knight then tipped the contents of the sack onto the bar.

'And one for my friend here!' he laughed. To our horror the sack contained a large orc head, severed just below the neck. It was with ever-increasing shock that we watched the landlord serve the head with ale, a smile on his lips.

'No charge of course for you, my lord,' he said, bowing low.

'Did you hear that?' Knobby whispered, his mouth wide open.

'Of course I bloody heard it,' I snapped.

'So what do you think?' Gilbert asked.

'I think we have a plan,' Knobby whispered with a wink.
'Right then, let's go find some horrible monster to kill!' I said, taking a long pull on our one mug of ale.
'Heroically, of course,' Boglith smiled.
So, finishing our ale, the four of us were once again on the move, this time looking not for a tavern, but some poor, harmless, unsuspecting, not-too-big monster to slay, ideally when it was fast asleep, or better still, already dead.

We travelled for two days without the slightest sight or sound of another living soul, let alone a monster that wanted to be slain. But then, on the eve of the third day, our luck changed; we came across our first monster. It was truly a terrible sight to behold. It must have towered four or five feet at the shoulder. Its massive bulk was shaded in large patches of black and white, two small horns pointed out from its head, and its unearthly cry filled the air.
'Mooo!' To the unwary traveller it must have looked a lot like a cow, just lying in the middle of the road, eating grass, looking at us, as cows tend to do.
'At last! Our first monster,' Knobby shouted triumphantly.
'What! We can't bravely go forth and slay a bloody cow,' I stammered.
'Of course we can,' Gilbert said.
'We could always say it was a demon cow that attacked travellers,' Knobby finished.
'Who in the name of seven bells is going to believe that this is a demon cow?' I said, pointing at the cow, which looked about to fall asleep.
'Moo.'
There was a long pause before Boglith spoke up. 'I'd believe that.'
'Yes, but you're an idiot!' I snapped.
'Look,' said Gilbert, walking me to the side of the road,

'what chance have we got against any real monsters? OK ... let's take a minute to think about this, shall we? On the one hand, you've got this monster-type-thing which probably isn't going to be a very nice kind of beastie, seeing as people want it dead, right?'

'Right.'

'And on the other hand, you've got the four of us, whose only weapon is a bottle-opener... So who would your money be on?'

'The monster,' I answered dejectedly.

'So that'll be us dead, then,' Knobby added, walking over.

'I guess so.'

'So, then, that's a demon cow,' Gilbert smiled, pointing at the cow.

'OK,' I sighed, 'if you say so, that's a terrorizing demon cow.'

'Great, then let's kill it!' shouted Knobby.

Drawing our one bottle opener, the four of us advanced on the waiting beast.

'Er... How do we do this, exactly?' Boglith asked.

'What? Well, we just, sort of ... er...' as I stood there looking at Boglith I realized that I hadn't got a clue how to kill a cow. As a village drunk that's not the sort of thing you're asked to do very often.

'Leave this to me,' Gilbert said, stepping forward.

'OK,' the three of us said in unison, stepping back.

Gilbert slowly moved forward, waving his arms about and muttering strange and arcane verses under his breath. When he was within a few yards of the beast, he slowly raised his arms to point at the cow – sorry, demon cow. All of a sudden the chanting stopped, and with a noise that can only be described as FUTZ, BANG, a bright blue fireball shot out of Gil's ring towards the oblivious animal. The whole effect was only slightly spoiled by the fact the fireball completely missed the cow and vanished beyond the horizon. The bang must have scared the cow, however, because it suddenly turned head on to us and charged in our direction. I looked at Knobby, and Boglith looked at Gil, and we all looked at the half a ton of pissed-off beef bearing down on us, and we all ran away. For almost an hour the now savage and very angry-looking cow chased the four of us brave adventurers along country lanes, until eventually giving up and sodding off back to greener pastures. As you may have guessed, we are not the world's fittest men, so by the time that animal stopped chasing us, we were exhausted, and were just slumped down where we stood, too knackered to take another step.

'Looks like a good place to stop,' Knobby whimpered.

As I crawled to the side of the road, the full horror of what had just happened hit me. Not only had we been chased by a farmyard animal, but we were still out of wine. Since no true hero would ever be seen running away from a cow, this meant – Oh God! – another night of Knobby's home-brew. At that moment, getting killed by the cow didn't seem that bad after all.

As the hazy sun began slowly to sink into the west, the four of us made camp. As the evening began to descend into darkness, a faint light could just be made out in the far distance.

'Look at that,' Knobby said, pointing to the strange glow in the distance, 'could be a camp fire.'

'Could be.'

'More trouble,' Boglith muttered under his breath.

'Come on, let's have a look,' Knobby urged.

'Nah ... I've just got this patch of mud nice and warm now,' I answered, not even looking at him.

As I lay there gazing up at the stars in the night sky, I could feel the mud slowly begin to ooze into my loincloth.

'You know, they might have wine,' Gilbert whispered.

That, and the feeling of cold wet mud seeping into the crack of my arse, was all the encouragement I needed to go have a look.

As we approached the source of the glow, what we discovered was not a small, welcoming camp fire, as we hoped, but four very dead, rather crispy-looking adventurers lying in the middle of the road. Their burnt and blackened bodies were beyond recognition, leaving only their charred armour and weapons, plus a few meagre supplies, intact. In fact, they looked for all the world as if they'd been hit by a large blue fireball shooting out of the sky. The smell of burning flesh hung heavy in the cool night air, forcing us to move away from the smoking remains.

'Well, at least you know where that fireball went,' Knobby said.

'Oh yeah! It landed us in deep shit,' moaned Boglith.

'But look on the bright side,' Gilbert chimed in, with a bright smile.

'What bright side? You've just crispy-fried four bloody people!'

'True ... but I missed the wine!' and with that he bent to pick up an undamaged wine sack from the remains.

'You don't want to touch that, it may be cursed from beyond the grave,' Boglith warned.

'What are you wittering on about?' Gilbert groaned.

'A friend of mine once drank a dead man's wine and in the morning he woke up with no penis.'

'By the gods! What was your friend's name?'

'Marion.'

'OK ... I think I can see the slight flaw in your story.'

'Well, don't say I didn't warn you.'

'OK, I won't,' said Gilbert, putting the wine sack to his lips. No sooner had the wine touched his lips than Gilbert froze, his eyes wide in terror. 'Oh no,' he whispered, slowly lowering the wine sack from his trembling lips.

'I told you!' Boglith cried, 'it's cursed.'
'What is it?'
'It's ... it's ... warm!'

As the night air grew chill, we sat huddled around the smouldering remains, enjoying the now mulled wine by the fading light of the fire. We investigated the few things Gilbert hadn't fried.

'Bloody hell, they've got some good shit here,' whispered Knobby, and so they had. Swords, helms and axes, armour and other supplies, all left untouched by Gilbert's small mistake, not to mention a rapidly depleting stock of wine. In fact they had all the things we'd forgotten to bring.

'So what do you think, guys?'

'I think we'll be keeping them,' answered Knobby, tucking a double-edged axe into his belt.

'You mean we just take them?' I asked.

'Of course ... if we don't, someone's just going to come along and steal this stuff,' Boglith answered, taking a sword.

'Someone like us?'

'Yeah ... but at least we had the good grace to kill them first,' Gilbert put in.

'OK then,' I sighed, as Knobby passed me a beautifully engraved broadsword.

So, that was the end of the argument. The next morning we all set out, looking like brave and strong heroes, which of course we were not.

4

Troll-ble Afoot

It was some five or six lonely days' march before we four brave and fearless-looking adventurers finally arrived at the next village; a small farming community on the border of the Black Head mountains, a place of dark legends and much darker deeds. The high snowy peaks were an abode of dragons, trolls, and other such nasty things, a place of ancient evil and patient malice, which many have entered but from which few have returned, which is why we were planning on going nowhere bloody near them.

As the four of us made our way into the village a strange thing occurred. The first villager we passed by jumped up and scurried away like a frightened rabbit. The second ran away screaming like a girl. The third just fainted right in front of us.

'I usually only have this effect on women!' Knobby joked.

'It's the smell,' whispered Gilbert.

The further we progressed into the village, the worse it became. Within minutes there seemed to be hundreds of limp villagers all over the bloody place.

'Something's wrong,' Boglith whispered.

'No shit ... people always faint when I walk around town,' I snapped.

'They know we've nicked this gear,' Boglith whispered.

'You think?' Knobby gasped, his eyes wide in terror.

'What's the mat...' I began, just before seeing the large, angry-looking mob marching right at us. I took a long look at Knobby, and Knobby took a long look at me. 'Leg it!' I suggested.

But by then it was far too late; the mob was almost on top of us. As we slowly tried to edge away from the crowd, while trying not to look as though we were, a small weather-beaten looking old man shoved his way to the front of the mob. Approaching us, he fell to his knees and began to wail: 'Oh thank the goddess ... you've come at last ... we'd almost lost all hope!' Rising once again to his feet, he turned to address the mob: 'At long last they have come, these brave souls who will slay the terror that has threatened us for so long.'

The crowd began to cheer wildly. As the cheers grew louder, Knobby turned to me saying, 'Slay the terror? ... that'll be us in deep shit, then.'

Slowly the cheering began to subside, and when the crowd at last grew silent the village chief handed me a large bag of gold.

As you said in your letter, half the gold in advance.' With that he pushed the large, bulging bag of golden coins into my hands. Knobby's greedy eyes bulged almost as much as the bag.

'Have no fear ... that monster's as good as dead!' Gilbert announced, stepping forward bravely and taking the gold, before anyone could shut him up.

'As we agreed, we have set aside a large room for you and your companions ... I hope this is adequate for your needs.'

'That'll be fine,' Knobby answered, stepping forward to snatch the gold from Gilbert's hands. As for me, all I could manage was to stand there opening and closing my mouth like a goldfish. My mind had not yet got past 'Slay the

terror', and I knew that Knobby was right; we really were in deep shit.
Less than an hour later the four of us were locked in our room above the village tavern and I was on the brink of losing my tiny mind. I paced the floor of our small room like a caged animal mumbling: 'What are we going to do ... what are we going to do?' until Knobby's booted foot made sharp contact with my testicles at high speed. I slowly crumpled to the floor, wishing I was dead, because as any man will tell you, given the choice between death and a kick to the balls, death wins every time.
'Thank you ... all that pacing was getting on my tits!' Knobby spat. Then as I lay on the floor crying, he sat down beside me. 'Now, if you've finished, I was about to tell you I have a cunning plan.'
'You could just have said so,' I croaked, painfully climbing on to one of the bunks.
'Yeah ... but where's the fun in that?' he smiled.
'So, what's your cunning plan, then?' I whimpered, lying down on the bed, still holding my testicles.
'We just wait until they're all asleep ... and this is the cunning part, then we run away. It'll be hours before they find out we're missing, and we'll be long gone by then!' he finished with an evil smile.
'I like it,' laughed Gilbert.
'Sounds good,' Boglith murmured.
'All right,' I agreed, 'anything to get out of this bleeding mess.'
The hours slowly ticked past, the tension grew, and we all waited patiently for the village to fall asleep. That is, the others did, but it wasn't long before I was happily snoring my head off.
The sun had long been chased from the sky by the time Knobby roused me.
'Wake up, you lazy bastard!' he snapped.

'Time to bugger off,' Gilbert smiled.

Creeping down the stairs, we found the whole tavern as quiet as a grave. In the dark street our every step seemed to echo in the silence, until we were sure someone would discover us. But with dawn only a few short hours away, we gratefully departed the village.

We hadn't got more than five minutes away when the heavens opened.

'Oh, shit, it's pissing it down.'

'That'll be us wet, then,' Knobby cursed.

For over an hour we trudged along in weather that would worry a duck, before deciding it was about time to find somewhere out of the rain to hide, if only so I could wring the water out of my loincloth. But it was another two hours, in the pouring rain, up to our knees in mud and mire, before we found the entrance to a huge menacing cave. The cave was dark and mysterious; wisps of grey vapour emanated from within. The stale smell of long-forgotten death hung heavily in the air. Basically, it was the sort of dark, menacing cave there is always a monster at the back of, in these kind of stories; but at least it was out of the rain.

'We're going in there?' Boglith asked.

'Let's just get inside and light a fire... This is getting too close to having a bath,' Knobby growled through gritted teeth, 'and I'm not due one for another twelve months!'

'That explains the smell,' said Gilbert, while the rest of us just nodded glumly.

Once inside, by the dim light of our small fire we got our first real look at our surroundings.

Are caves supposed to have green carpets?' Boglith asked.

The cave floor was covered in a bright green carpet, on which our little fire was now merrily burning a very large hole.

'Oh my God ... look at that!' Gilbert gasped.

'What?' I asked, looking wildly around the cave.
'Those curtains really don't match this carpet!'

It only then that I noticed that just a few things seemed a little out of place. For one thing I was pretty sure that most normal caves didn't come with bright green carpet and purple curtains. Then there was the large 'Home Sweet Home' sign, nailed to the far wall, and the small matter of the huge pink, fluffy slippers on the floor – not to mention the very angry-looking rock troll who was wearing the aforementioned slippers.

Now, at this point, I feel I should explain a little about the nature of rock trolls. They are one of the most evil races in the lands around the mountains. They are cruel, black-hearted and crude. If you should encounter a rock troll, the best thing to do is run away extremely quickly. The best way to piss off a rock troll, apparently, is to burn a large hole in his bright green carpet. But before I could persuade my feet to get out of there, all hell broke loose. Gilbert panicked and let loose another one of his famous blue fireballs, right at the troll. As usual, his aim was just a little on the bad side of awful and the fireball completely missed the troll and smashed into the ceiling of the cave, spraying the cave with bright blue fire. As the fire quickly spread to the troll's nice blue wallpaper and purple curtains, he lumbered to his feet, grabbing a rather nasty-looking sword from the side of the sofa. As he advanced towards us, his long, greasy hair caught on the fiery curtains, and in seconds his whole head was ablaze. Dropping the sword, the troll tried desperately to put out his flaming head by running around and slapping it; tripped over his large slippers, and crashed to the floor of the cave – knocked out cold, or as cold as you can get with your head on fire. Within a few short minutes the whole tasteless cave was aflame, the air filled with a choking black smoke and the strange smell of roasting rock troll.

'You think it's dead?' Knobby asked, retreating from the flames.

'No, I think it's just having a lie-down ... Who the hell cares? Let's just get the hell out of here!'

As we approached the mouth of the cave, the first thing we saw was a large mob gathered around it, looking in. There seemed to be rather a lot of them waiting for us.

'That'll be us caught, then,' Knobby announced.

'Could this day get any worse?' I groaned.

'Look on the bright side,' Gilbert shrugged.

'What bright side?'

'I have absolutely no idea ... but if you find one, let me know.'

With nowhere to run we had little choice but to stand our ground and await the mob. As they approached, cheering began, and to our amazement we were carried shoulder-high back to the village.

Now, if you're a little confused as to what was going on, let me explain. The rock troll that we had so bravely slain, was in fact the same monster that had been terrorizing the village, wandering about there and demanding that the villagers try his cooking; anyone that wouldn't, he used as ingredients for his next dish.

5

Lud

The next couple of weeks passed by in a drunken haze, an endless orgy of wine, women and song, interrupted only by the occasional visit to the bathroom. We were the saviours of the village, heroes at last. We were welcomed back with riotous joy and jubilation, not to mention more than a few drinks. A large room was given over to the four of us. The party never ended. The taverns were always open, as were the tavern girls. I even heard a rumour that Knobby, yes, Knobby, managed to get lucky, but, of course, he did have to pay for it. Life was good ... that was, until one fateful Monday morning.

The party the night before had been particularly riotous. I had ended up trying to chat up the barman, a large, angry man named Colin, and Knobby had ended up sleeping with a very shocked Colin. I had just fallen out of bed that morning and was quite happy lying face down on the floor, allowing the blood to gently flow, when the knocking began. At first I just lay there, unsure whether the knocking was coming from outside or inside my head. It was quite a while before I yanked the door open, ready to inflict great pain on the bastard knocking on my door so early. As I hauled the door open I came face to forehead with the elder of the village.

'There's someone here to see you ... a woman,' he announced, bowing low. 'Please follow me.'

'Is it OK if I put my pants on first?' I asked, and struggling into my breeches, I hopped along behind him to the stairs. No matter what they say, you cannot hop downstairs with your trousers round your ankles, so, at the bottom of the stairs, picking myself up from on top of the now very squashed elder, I pulled my trousers up just in time as the others walked in.

'What's going on?' I asked.

'Buggered if I know ... hey, is he all right?' Knobby asked, pointing to the bleeding village elder.

'I just fell downstairs on top of him.'

'We'd better help him,' Boglith urged, rushing forward.

'What! Yeah, all right.'

As we helped the crushed elder back to his feet, the tavern doors swung open to admit one of the most beautiful creatures I had ever seen. Part lady, part goddess ... and all woman. In a short leather tunic worn high on the hips to reveal long tanned legs and an arse to die for, this nymph would have made any man forget his own name. A loud crash made me turn round and I saw what was left of the village elder, now lying on his face back at the bottom of the stairs, where Knobby and Boglith had dropped him.

'My lords, I need your help,' purred the goddess, in a voice as sweet as honey.

'Umm...' I moaned, sporting a moronic grin. Mistaking my horny grunts as a rebuff, she fell on her knees, pleading. 'Oh please help me, my lords. You are my only hope.'

'Uhhh ...' I mumbled, incapable of moving my eyes from her ample cleavage.

'My people are in grave danger ... we are being terrorized by an evil dragon.'

Before any of us could stop him, once again Gilbert stepped right in. 'Have no fear ... sorry, I don't know your name.'

'Iggly,' she answered, rewarding him with a dazzling smile.

'Iggly. That's a very beautiful name,' he smiled, leaning forward. 'Yes, sorry, have no fear, we'll save your village!'

'Gilbert, may we have a quiet word with you?' I asked.

Later, when we all stepped into the street, Gilbert sporting a black eye, we found it packed with people; it was as if the whole village had turned out to see us off. As the cheering crowd parted in front of us, my heart sank. Iggly was astride a large black horse and, to my horror, another four bloody big horses were tied up outside the tavern for us.

You are so bloody dead it's untrue,' I snapped at the cringing Gilbert.

'A horse,' Knobby gasped. 'I can't ride a sodding horse.'

'Come on, don't be such an arse,' I laughed.

'It's not my arse I'm worried about, it's my face,' Knobby answered.

'Your face?'

'Yes, my bloody face as that's what is going to smash into the floor the second I get on that bleeding thing,' he spat.

'But with a face like yours, mate, how would we tell the difference between that and your arse anyway?' Gilbert laughed.

It was true though, falling off was easy, very easy in fact. Poor Knobby's face hit the dirt so often it was beginning to look like a paving slab. No matter how much you try, you can't get a four-foot angry dwarf on to a six-foot horse; it just won't work. After what seemed like an age of watching him climb on and fall off, some kind soul managed to find him a small pack mule to ride. It seemed all the funnier, however, when he fell off that.

'I've got an idea,' Boglith smiled.

The sun was fast approaching noon by the time we managed

to tie Knobby on to the mule and, with many a loud curse from the incensed dwarf, we were at last on our way.

The hazy light of dusk was slowly beginning to darken by the time we called a halt for the day. As I untied the now furious Knobby, Iggly set about making camp for the night. As for the others, they just stood around trying to rub some feeling back into their arses. The heavy night sky fell into deepening darkness, and the five of us stood (not one of us could sit down at that moment) around the welcoming fire. Fatigue weighed heavy on us and it wasn't long before Iggly stumbled off to her blankets.

'Now what?' Knobby whispered.

'Umm...'

'How the hell are we going to get out of this?'

'How am I supposed to know? Ask him, this was his brilliant idea.'

'Look, how many more times can I say I'm sorry?' Gilbert sighed.

'A lot,' we all seemed to snap together.

'OK, sorry ... Now do you feel better?'

'Oh yeah! We're all going to die horribly, but now you've said sorry, I feel a lot better ... you prat!' Knobby snapped.

'Look, just calm down,' Gilbert said. 'We just wait until she falls asleep and run away.'

'Oh! Because that worked so well last time,' Knobby growled.

'Well, have you got any bright ideas?'

'As it happens I haven't,' Knobby answered.

'Well, then...'

'Tell me about your adventures,' Iggly interrupted, rising from her blankets and walking over to us. 'Heroes like yourselves must have many a story to tell.'

'Oh yeah, hundreds,' I answered.

'Will you tell me some?' she smiled, in that way that only women can, so you've got no chance to say no.

'Well, let me see ... there was the time we had that terrible battle with that two-headed monster with the big ... er .. er.'

'Teeth!' Knobby added triumphantly.

'Yeah, and don't forget those dreadful claws on those ... those...'

'Arms,' Gilbert interrupted.

'Yeah, that battle seemed to last for days,' Knobby mused.

'That's where I got this scar,' Gilbert said, pointing to his head.

'What scar?' Iggly asked, staring hard at his forehead.

'Well, you can't see it in this light, of course.'

'And of course there was the last time we fought and killed a dragon...' But Boglith had to stop there as something hit him across the back of the head.

'Oh, please tell me about that, my lords,' she pleaded, this time turning on the eyelashes, so we had no chance.

'Urr ... um ... Knobby!' I gurgled.

'Oh yeah ... ah ... Boglith?' Knobby choked.

'Oh ... Gilbert, how about you tell her?'

'Er, well, that was horrendous. For hours we battled with the fierce monster; must have been larger than ten houses. Its fiery breath could incinerate a grown man in scant seconds, but we won, so that was OK. Anyway, how long till we get to your village?'

'Oh, not long, we should be there by late tomorrow.'

'Do you know where the dragon is?' I asked.

'Oh yes, its cave isn't far from our village.'

'Great ... so we'll be there tomorrow. That's just great.' Knobby grimaced.

'I have a surprise for you, my lords ... you'll see what it is tomorrow.'

'What sort of surprise?' Knobby asked.

'Oh – a big surprise, my lords, something that will help in your quest to slay the dragon and save our village.'

'Something that will help us to slay the dragon?' Knobby repeated.
'Yes.'
'But not actually slay the dragon?'
'No!'
'Right ... thought so.'
'Well, exciting as all this is, I'm bollocked,' I groaned, stumbling for my blankets.

The following morning dawned misty, with just a hint of rain and, for the first time in years, without a hangover. But this was just the start of the truly awful day to come. The ride was a nightmare, and by the time we arrived at Iggly's village my arse was red raw and my balls felt like they'd been used as a punch bag.

Iggly's village was small, tumbledown, and obviously in the savage grip of some terrible evil. The whole village seemed to wear defeat like a cloak. It was probably the most depressing place on earth; you could tell they were in really deep shit.

'There's someone I want you to meet,' Iggly cried, leaping from her horse and skipping away.

'Can't wait,' Boglith sighed.

As we untied a very unhappy Knobby, Iggly came running back around the corner with one of the biggest men I had ever seen in my life. He must have stood well over seven feet tall, bloated blue veins pulsating over his massive frame, with a jaw you could break rocks on. Wearing little more than a small loincloth, that you could tell his religion through, and one sodding big sword, he scared the living shit out of me.

'My lords, this is my surprise. Allow me to introduce Lud the Destroyer!'

'So, what do you do, then?' Knobby asked, rubbing the feeling back into his swollen arse.

'Umm...'
'Lud is the village's greatest warrior!' Iggly smiled.
'Whoopee!' Boglith sighed.
'He will take you to the dragon's cave, and go in with you.'
'That'll be nice,' Knobby whispered.
'Oh, that's lovely ... Lud is so excited, aren't you, Lud?' she cried, clapping her hands.
'Uggh,' the massive frame muttered.
'Your rooms above the tavern are ready and waiting for you. I've arranged for the landlord to wake you before first light.'

As night began to fall we once again found ourselves above a strange tavern, and for the second time I had entered the realms of total panic. Just place me in danger of being killed, hurt, maimed, or even poked with a stick, and like any red-blooded coward I'll panic.

'By all the gods, for pity's sake, stop bloody panicking,' Knobby snapped.

'I like bloody panicking,' I shouted.

'I've got an idea,' Boglith murmured.

'What?' I snapped, pacing past him.

'This,' said Boglith, his boot smashing into my testicles once again.

As the searing pain in my groin began to subside, I discerned the dulcet tones of Knobby, talking to the others.

'Listen, what have we got to lose?'

'Just our arses,' Boglith whimpered.

'Look, we just let old muscles downstairs do all the donkey work, and we take all the credit!'

'I just don't see why we can't all run away again,' I choked from the floor.

'Because we always bollocks it up,' Gilbert snapped.

'So, what happens if something happens to Lud?' I asked.

'Then we run away,' Gilbert smiled.

'Right into another pile of shit,' Boglith sighed.

'So we're agreed then – we all go along with Lud for now?' Gilbert asked.

'Yes.'

'Yes.'

'No.' But no one was listening to my pitiful moans from the floor.

That night my sleep was somewhat disturbed. I never seem to sleep well just before I'm about to die horribly.

6

This could be Orc-ward

Next morning found the five of us standing outside the tavern, and it seemed the whole village had turned out to see us off – all twenty-four of them. With the harsh light of dawn cresting the savage Black Head mountains to the west, we set off on our lonely quest towards certain incineration. It was not long before we discovered just how valuable Lud was as a travelling companion. For one thing, he never rode, so we could leave those arse-numbing horses behind. He also seemed to carry rather a large amount of fine wine hidden about his person, which greatly endeared him to all of us.

We made camp that night by the banks of a shallow river. Lud lit a small fire, and we sat around enjoying the night air and toasting Lud's health.

Then, as the pale moon rose to its zenith and the small clearing was bathed in blue light, we were able to see clearly two rather ugly orcs with drawn swords, advancing towards us.

'Nice fire, humans,' they snarled.

Without a word, Lud was upon them. A loud crunching noise rent the air as Lud's powerful knee met the first orc's testicles and as his helpless form fell to earth, Lud grabbed the back of his greasy hair. The noise that followed brought tears to my eyes; in one swift movement Lud bit the back of the orc's head, separating it from the rest of its body. Through the whole encounter the second small orc had just stood, transfixed, but now, as the massive bloodstained form of Lud advanced on him, he gave a sort of quiet choking noise and fell to the ground, dead. Lud had literally scared the poor bastard to death. Stripping them of gold, Lud carried the limp forms to the edge of the camp, and threw them into the river.

'Not bad, not bad,' said Knobby.

'A bit slow, perhaps?' Gilbert asked.

'A bit too messy,' Boglith said, gazing at the blood-soaked Lud.

'Oh, I'm sorry. You didn't want to kill them, did you?' Lud asked.

'No, no. You did just fine, my boy,' Knobby answered with a smile.

'Yeah, pretty good,' Gilbert nodded. 'Of course, we would have done it quicker, but you weren't bad.'

'But you're real heroes. I'm just a warrior,' Lud said, squatting down by the fire.

'Don't worry, you'll get there, Lud my lad,' Knobby smiled, clapping Lud on the back. 'Why, some day you'll be great hero!'

'Oh no, I could never be as great as you, my lords,' Lud answered, far too seriously for my liking.

'Oh, greater,' Knobby answered, reddening.

An uncomfortable silence settled on the group.

'So, Lud ... How long before we get to this little dragon of yours, then?' I asked.

'Oh, we should arrive at One-Hundred-and-Forty-Two some time early tomorrow.'

'Why do you call it One-Hundred-and-Forty-Two?' Boglith asked with a drunken smile.

'That's the number of men it's slain in the past year,' Lud answered.

'You had to bloody ask,' Gilbert sighed, glaring at the elf.

'Who keeps count?' Boglith asked.

'It's written in blood outside the cave,' Lud replied nonchalantly.

'Oh, that's helpful,' I mused.

'I need a large drink,' Knobby said, reaching for the wine bottle. 'Smoke?' he offered, fishing his pipe out of his pack.

'No thanks,' I answered.

Now, it's a little known fact that dwarves have long nasal hairs, something my short, drunken friend should have remembered, for as he bent close to the fire to light his pipe, his whole nose went up like a firework. Something about the sight of Knobby running around trying to put out his flaming nose turned my thoughts to the prospect ahead of us.

The next morning Lud caught breakfast in a way that I really don't want to talk about very much, but suffice it to say that it involved a piece of string, an empty bottle of wine, and one very surprised-looking stag.

With a whole stag roasting over our small fire, we decided to spend the rest of the day resting, feasting and, of course, drinking Lud's wine, to prepare for our ordeal ahead. By nightfall, a cool breeze had dissipated the sweet smell of roasting stag, and we lay close to the fire, our stomachs tight and our eyes greedy.

'You know the trouble with too much wild venison?' Knobby asked, stuffing yet another huge piece of roast stag into his mouth.

'What?'

'After a while it can taste a little stagnant!'

By the time the moon reached its zenith we were well and truly drunk again, and curled up by the fire. Within minutes I fell asleep.

* * *

'Wake up – will you *please* wake up, you bastard!' Knobby shouted, shaking me awake; though his rancid breath was enough to wake the dead all by itself.

'What?' I moaned, turning over and trying to go back to sleep.

'Will you wake up! The dragon's got Lud!' Knobby screamed.

'Mmm...' I was trying my very best to pull my blanket over my head.

'The dragon's got Lud!' he repeated, this time right into my left ear.

'Who got who?'

'The dragon's eaten Lud!'

'Who's eaten? Is breakfast ready?'

'The dragon!' he shouted, flapping his stubby arms. 'He's taken Lud! He's got the bloody wine!'

In the remains of my hungover brain, the disastrous news managed to sink in.

'Oh ... my ... God,' I stammered, struggling to my feet. 'We've got to look for him.'

It was at this point that Lud walked back into camp.

'Time to go,' he announced, with a bright smile.

I felt an amazing sense of relief as my hands clamped around Knobby's throat, only to have it ruined by Boglith and Gilbert dragging me off. So, recovering my shattered composure, I just kicked him in the testicles instead. Packing our few belongings away, we picked up the squealing ball of dwarf, and started once again on our way. As the miles slowly passed, a small but niggling doubt began to assail me.

'Lud, are we out of wine?' I asked, fearing the terrible answer.

'Yeah,' he answered, with a shrug. With that one word my world tumbled into darkness, and all hope failed.

36

It was getting dark by the time I came round, and I wished I hadn't. I was face to face with the entrance to the dragon's cave. Struggling up onto shaky feet, I got my first real look inside. It was dark and cold, wisps of thin grey vapour drifted out; I had the impression of a giant waiting grave. I don't mind admitting it scared the shit out of me. We all stood there, gazing into the jaws of inevitable death, and knew that this whole bloody mess was Gilbert's fault. Terror took hold of my clenched bowels, all eyes turned to Gilbert and, as an overpowering smell wafted towards him, he fainted.

'Sorry about that,' I mumbled, waving my hand behind me, 'too many beans last night!'

7

The Dragon

Slowly coming to, Gilbert looked at the grim faces around him, his jaw dropping lower by the second, and realization began to dawn on him. His eyes wide with terror, he searched desperately for a means of escape; he didn't find one. Only then the full stupidity of his actions sank in: not only were we going to die in appalling agony, but it was all his flaming fault. Three things helped him come to this conclusion. The first was the wide-eyed look of utter terror all his friends now wore, that seemed to say: We're not just afraid, we bloody smell afraid. The second was a discarded lance propped up outside the entrance to the cave, a large piece of decaying flesh attached to the pointy end, looking for all the world like some very big toothpick; and judging by the size of what was attached to the lance, it had picked some pretty big teeth. Third, there was Lud. There stood a man-monster well over seven feet tall, who had, just days ago, bitten the head off one orc, and literally scared another to death. This mountain of a man, this brick shithouse, was standing there, transfixed, looking more than a little worried.

But perhaps more disturbing than any of these sights was a small sign nailed to the cave entrance, which announced in faultless copperplate writing: FREE SMALL KITTENS. APPLY WITHIN.

'It's just not my day,' thought Gilbert as he passed out once again. There was no way we were walking into that cave carrying a spark-out wizard. We needed Gilbert for the dragon to eat first, while we ran away. But by the time Gilbert finally came round the moon had long since risen and since none of us wanted to be fried at night, we decided it would be nicer to die horribly in the morning instead, which also gave us longer to come up with a plan to get out of this. Not that any of us did, except Knobby. As morning broke on what was undoubtedly our last day on earth, we all took a few seconds to realize that Knobby had run away in the night. We found him with two bits of twig stuck in his hair, sitting under a tree pretending to be a bush, a disguise that would have had us all fooled if he hadn't said hello as we walked past.

The five of us united again, we prepared to enter the abode of the dragon. By the pale light of dawn it didn't look a lot better; in fact it looked worse. I couldn't get my feet to move in its direction, till with the help of a kick in my arse from the short one I went staggering into the cave. Once inside my fears began to swell. The deepening darkness seemed to dislike being disturbed; it crowded in from all sides; a veil seemed to fall across our eyes. I could only just make out the lumbering form of Lud, just before I walked into him.

'I'll light a torch,' he announced.

As the torch flared we got our first good look at the dragon's cave; blood smeared the walls and floor; it was like walking into hell itself.

'I'll wait for you guys outside,' Knobby said, turning to run down the passage.

'Let's go on,' Lud said, picking Knobby up by the collar.

With his legs flailing desperately, the helpless Knobby was carried down the passage. By the flickering light of the torch I could just make out the shadowy entrances of other passages branching off on all sides. Lud never paused; he just kept marching straight ahead, looking neither left nor right. It began to dawn on me that Lud knew exactly where he was going. The bastard was taking us right to the dragon.

'Hey, Lud, you got any idea where you're going?' I asked, trying to force a smile.

'Kill dragon!' he shouted, putting Knobby down and waving his sword above his head.

'The bastard's taking us right to King Barbecue!' I whispered to Knobby.

'Let's kill Lud and run away,' Knobby whispered back.

'Oh yeah. And how do we do that, pray tell? Do you remember those orcs at all?' Gilbert asked, with a raised eyebrow.

'You got any better ideas?' I asked.

'Look, all we have to do is wait for the right moment, then run away. Like when the dragon's eating our friend there,' Gilbert answered, pointing to Lud.

So we continued trudging along in the deepening darkness, just waiting for the right moment to do a runner. The further we marched into the gloom, the more appealing the idea of killing Lud and running away became.

It was poor old Boglith, now, for some reason, at the front of the party, who broke my chain of thought. 'You know,' he began, 'these sorts of places are always full of ... raaaaaps!' he screamed, disappearing into a hole in the floor.

'That'll be a trap then,' Knobby added.

'Excuse me ... HELP!' echoed up from the hole.

Peering down into the darkness, we could just make out the dangling form of the elf, some feet below us.

'Boggy mate, you've fallen down a large hole,' I shouted down to him.

'Please get me out of here!'

With Lud's help, as he was the only one of us who had remembered to bring any rope, we winched the helpless elf out.

'I didn't know you had found religion,' Knobby smiled, as Boglith climbed over the edge of the pit.

'What!' Boglith asked, dusting himself off.

'Well, you've come over all holy.' Knobby laughed.

We once again marched into the heart of the mountain; but this time, we all walked along staring at the floor ahead.

The nearer we came to the centre of the mountain, the hotter it seemed to become. It was a stifling kind of heat that made breathing unbearable. As the heat grew, so did the light, until the walls of the passage seemed to radiate a warm orange glow. All in all, I was getting more than a little worried with each step I took. Before long we came to a crossroads, at which Lud paused to catch his breath. As for the rest of us, we were too shagged to catch anything, so we just sat on the floor and waited.

'Do you get dandruff?' Knobby asked, scratching his greasy mane.

'Only on my bikini line. Why do you ask?'

'Oh, it's just all this white powder,' he answered, showing me a handful of white dust.

By the faint light of Lud's torch I could just make out a thin layer of fine white powder covering everything.

'I think we should...' Lud began to say, when a giant torrent of white flame sprang from the left-hand passage, vaporising Lud in seconds, leaving behind only a few puffs of smoke and a small pile of white powder on the floor where he had been standing.

'That'll be the dragon, then!' shouted Knobby, as his arse disappeared down the passage, closely followed by mine.

It is at times like this that you realize just how important friends can be. I mean, if you're lucky, while the dragon's eating them, you can escape.

'Now would be a good time to run away,' Gilbert shouted, sprinting past me.

Just when I was beginning to think we were safe, another tongue of fire swept up behind us. With flames licking against my arse, I saw a side passage; diving face first into it we just avoided being fried, as a huge gout of flame consumed the whole passage. My mouth full of dirt, I watched it roar past the entrance to our tunnel; my clothes were smouldering, Knobby's arse in flames.

'What do we do now?' Boglith asked, after we had finished stamping out Knobby's arse.

'How about getting the hell out of here?' Gilbert suggested.

'I don't know about you, but I don't fancy going back out there,' I said, pointing back down the passage.

'Well, let's see where this passage leads, then.'

Without another word it was back into the darkness. In a strange way it was almost comforting; no red glow meant no dragon, so it would be a little while before we all died in agony. With no Lud and no hope of rescue we began our long walk into the unknown. Every step seemed to take us deeper and deeper into the mountain. Now, without the help of Lud's torch, the darkness seemed to rush in from all sides; I tried waving my hand in front of my face, but I really could see nothing.

'Dark, ain't it?' whispered Knobby.

Just then a blood-curdling scream rent the air, echoing down the passage and sending a shiver down my spine.

'What's that?' I yelled, jumping back and scrambling for my sword.

'Oh shit ... it's bloody me,' moaned Gilbert, 'I've just smashed my dick on a bleeding doorknob.'

'What were you doing at the time?' Boglith asked.

'I just walked into it.'

'What's a doorknob doing in the middle of a passage?'

'It's on a sodding door, what do you think?'

'OK then, I repeat, what's a door doing in the middle of a dark passage?'

'It's at the end of the tunnel, you prat.'

'Well, don't just stand there rubbing your knob – open the door.'

In the end it took all four of us to open the door. After ten minutes pushing and shoving, the door still hadn't budged.

'Bugger me,' Knobby gasped, slumping to the floor, and at these words, as if by magic the door swung open.

The room on the other side was bathed in soft, gentle light. The walls and ceiling were decorated in ornate carvings, so that not a bare patch of wall could be seen. The floor was covered in pale, bloodstained carpet; not the best of signs. The only furniture was a small, battered, three-legged stool in a corner. A large, black wooden door on the opposite side of the room was the only means of escape.

'Oh, thank the gods for that,' Boglith sighed, stumbling towards the stool, 'I could do with a sit-down.'

Suddenly the room was filled with a scream of pure terror; the second Boglith's arse hit the stool two large wooden arms sprang out from beneath the seat and were now holding the horrified elf in place. But Boglith's eyes bulged in terror as the stool then began to grow a far more dreadful magical appendage, and bouncing violently up and down, started raping the helpless elf. Boglith's screams filled the room as he was rogered by the sadistic stool.

'HELP! HELP! HELP!' echoed round the room as the crazed stool bounced faster and faster.

'Kill it! Kill it! Oh God, please kill it!' the victim screamed.

Drawing our weapons we began hacking away at the

demon chair, but to no avail. The sharpest sword and the heaviest axe left not a mark; we watched the lifeless form of Boglith bounce around the room. After what felt like an age the bouncing began to slow, until finally coming to a shuddering halt. The magic arms then slowly withdrew and the limp form of Boglith slid to the floor. As we rushed over and picked up the gibbering wreck that was once Boglith, I noticed a small, torn piece of paper tacked to the underside of the seat. Upon it was written the legend:

WARNING. STOOL OF BUGGERY.
DO NOT TOUCH, AND YOU REALLY
DON'T WANT TO SIT DOWN.

'You OK, mate?' I asked, as we put a new pair of trousers on the elf.

'How you feeling?' Gilbert asked.

'Oh, bloody great. Just fantastic for someone that's just been raped by a chair.' He kicked the now inanimate stool. 'Now can we please get the hell out of here, or would anyone else like to take a seat?' and he stormed off towards the door.

At this, the stool once again seemed to come alive. With one bound it was halfway across the room at Boglith's side, almost like a faithful old dog. An evil smile slowly spread across Boglith's face.

'Oh all right then, you can come,' he said to it.

'What!' we gasped as one. 'After what that bloody thing's done to you?'

'I know, I know, but at least I've got something for Silmare's birthday now!' And with a broad smile he turned back towards the door.

A lot larger than the first, this door was carved out of dark ebony; warm to the touch, it seemed almost comforting, until I realised what was most probably on the other side.

'It's locked,' Boglith announced, wiggling the knob.

'Oh, what a shame. We'll just have to find another way out,' I said, heading for the other door.

'No ... I think I can open this,' Gilbert said, groping around in his underwear.

'My God, what the hell are you going to open it with?'

'Relax ... lock pick,' he announced, producing a small silk pouch from his loincloth. It took him less than thirty seconds to open the door.

'Too much time spent getting into the girls' locker rooms at wizard school!' he said with a wry smile, as the door swung open with a rusty creak.

The room on the other side was much larger than the first; dark and musty, the rancid smell of death hung heavily in the still air. On the far wall a rusty iron door stood slightly ajar, and above this a large sign hung, upon which, written in blood, were the words: DEATH AWAITS ALL WITHIN!

'Who's for going back another way, then?' Knobby whispered, turning to leave.

'Look at this,' Gilbert shouted.

On the left-hand wall a single word had been scrawled in blood: HOARD, it read. Just below the sign was a disconcerting heap of human bones and a small pile of golden coins. To the right of the bloody mess was a small green door, about eleven inches high, with a small 'Home Sweet Home' sign nailed over it. By the right-hand wall was the corpse of the last poor soul to have made it this far. Huge talon marks scored the upper body; arms hung from torn ligaments; of the head there was no sign. All in all, not the prettiest of pictures. As we all stood around open-mouthed, wondering what to do next, the small green door swung open and a small brownie walked in, stark naked, carrying a bottle of wine. Seeing us the brownie dropped his wine and grabbed a tiny sword, which looked suspiciously like a big pin.

'Who are y-y-you? W-w-what are you d-d-d-doing here?' he stuttered. 'F-f-flee now, or you will be d-d-destr... Sod it ... you'll be hurt a lot!'

'Look, that's just what we're trying...' But before Gilbert had a chance to finish, the brownie darted forward and with a shout of 'Have at thee!' stabbed him in the toe, and darted back through the little door.

'Little sod!' Gil shouted, and with a scream of rage and fury tore open the second door, only to come face to snout with one bloody big son-of-a-bitch dragon, wisps of smoke and flame sprouting from its gaping maw. Giant red and purple scales covered its massive form, huge claws dug furrows in the cave floor. You could hear Gilbert's nerve go from across the other side of the room, and you could have smelt it go about a mile away.

'WHO D-D-DARES TO D-D-DISTURB MY SLUMBER?' boomed the dragon.

'That'll be us dead, then,' Knobby whispered.

'COME OUT AND F-F-FACE ME!' it growled. 'D-D-DO YOU HAVE ANY LAST W-W-WORDS?' it growled.

'Er, yes, I have one!' I whispered.

'WHAT?'

'HELP!' I screamed at the top of my voice.

'NOW PREPARE TO D-D-DIE!' it boomed.

I stood there, awaiting my fiery end, but seconds passed with no sign of any flame. I had time to notice one or two things that seemed a little out of place. The first was that bloody stutter, which sounded an awful lot like that brownie we'd just met. Another was that the dragon's mouth never seemed to move when it spoke. Now that I thought about it, the whole flaming dragon didn't move a muscle. Then there was that terrible smell; I wasn't sure that any living thing could smell *that* bad. It was as if a hundred years of death and decay hung in the air. Finally, there was the matter of the small green door. I felt almost positive that dragons don't have little doors in their legs, but this one did.

'Wait a minute, you're that bloody brownie, aren't you?' I shouted.

'NO, I'M NOT,' boomed the dragon.

'Yes, you are! You're that little brownie.'

'NO, I'M A D-D-DRAGON, HONEST. I'M A TERRIBLE MAN-EATING D-D-DRAGON.'

'No, you're not!' I answered.

'YES, I AM! T-T-TREMBLE IN F-F-FEAR! P-P-PREPARE TO F-F-FRY!' boomed the dragon.

'What about the door in your leg?' I asked.

'IGNORE THE DOOR. F-F-FLEE NOW AND I MAY SPARE YOU!'

'God, will you please come out of there,' Gilbert shouted, kicking the small door in the dragon's leg. There was a long pause before the dragon again spoke.

'NO. YOU'LL HURT ME.'

'Of course we won't hurt you,' I said.

'YOU PROMISE?'

'We promise,' we all said together.

After what seemed like an age the small door slowly swung open, and one very sheepish-looking, naked brownie emerged.

'Now listen, I am sorry about all th –'

'Little bastard!' Gilbert interrupted, stamping on the helpless imp, leaving only two small arms and legs sticking out from beneath his boot.

'Now can we please get the hell out of here before we come across any real bleeding dragon,' I muttered.

'Wait a minute,' Knobby said, drawing his axe. Striding forward, he chopped the head off the stuffed dragon with one fluid motion – or ten minutes hacking, if you want to be honest.

'Might as well get paid for all this,' he said, lifting the dragon's head over his shoulder.

'Who's to know we didn't kill the flaming thing?' Boglith smiled.

'Underhand, crafty ... I like it!' Gilbert smiled.

We gathered up all the gold, and anything else we could find, and started on our way back down the passage, our ever-faithful stool by our side. It must have taken a little more than an hour to find our way back to the main passage.

'What's all this bloody dust?' Boglith asked.

'That'll be our Lud, then!' Knobby smiled.

We didn't go much further, but sat in the darkness of the tunnel and shed a small tear for the loss of Lud, and his wine.

8

Brownie Trousers

As I am sure you know, dwarves and elves can see almost perfectly in the dark, unlike us poor humans, who have mostly only mastered the art of walking into things and saying Sorry. Given enough time, however, even our eyes will adjust to darkness, and after spending so many hours lost in those tunnels, when we finally approached the light we just stood, blinking in the harsh light of day. The air smelt clean and fresh, and the world slowly shifted back into focus.

But the sight that met our eyes was not a pleasant one. It seemed the whole brownie nation had turned out to greet us. There must have been thousands of the little bastards for, as far as the eye could see, it was wall-to-wall, loincloth-to-loincloth, homicidal midgets. It was not unlike a party at Knobby's house, in fact.

'Now you've put your foot in it,' Knobby whispered to Gilbert.

'Look, just watch your step,' I added.

At this point I feel I should explain a little about the brownie race in general. Brownies are by nature cruel, heartless, hot-headed and aggressive, one of the most unpleasant races in all the lands – not that this is too much of a problem, as your average brownie is nine inches high. Even small kittens are a hazard to them, so brownies have learnt to hunt in large packs; bloody large packs, in fact.

'It's a damn shame you bastards ate my cat,' Gil whispered.

'You said it was chicken,' Boglith said, confronting Gilbert.

'Of course it wasn't bloody chicken. What the hell did you expect?'

'I expected, when you said, have some chicken, not to be eating your flaming cat!' Boglith snapped.

'Er, excuse me!' a voice from low down squeaked.

'Well, you ate it, anyway.'

'That's because I thought it was bloody chicken!'

'Well, I thought it tasted just purrfect,' Knobby smiled.

'Oh shut up,'

'EXCUSE ME!' the head brownie shouted, jumping up and down on the spot.

'Oh yeah, sorry.'

'Now, when you good gentlemen are quite finished...'

'Sorry about that,' I said.

'Can we get down to business? By the way you haven't got anything furry with you, by any chance?' the brownie asked.

'Only the dwarf.'

'But no kittens?'

'No,' I answered.

'Good. Not that I was worried, you understand, I was just asking,' he lied. Then, turning back to his people, he shouted, 'The brownie people gives thanks for your bravery in slaying this evil.'

'Hey, any time,' Gilbert smiled, stepping forward, narrowly avoiding stepping on the head brownie.

'It's only a shame our great King could not be here to see this day,' the brownie continued. At his words, the whole of the brownie nation seemed to hang their heads in sorrow.

'Now, let us lead you back to your village for the welcome you so richly deserve.'

'Lead on then,' Knobby smiled.

We had not gone more than a few steps when the head brownie, now sitting on Boglith's foot, spoke again.

'Many long years ago, our great King ventured into those accursed caves, never to be seen again. Tell me truly, did you see owt of our King?'

'Oh yes. Is that him?' Gilbert asked, raising his boot to show the squashed remains of the brownie King.

There seemed, now, little more the rest of us could do but hang our heads in shame and await the worst. It wasn't long coming. It took a few short seconds for Gilbert's actions to sink in but, when they did, the head brownie completely lost control.

'KILL THEM! KILL THEM! KILL THEM! KILL THEM NOW!' he screamed, jumping off Boglith's foot.

A groan went up, and in seconds we were completely surrounded and being peppered by thousands of tiny arrows.

'Run!' Knobby shouted.

Needing no second invitation, we made a break for it, trampling brownies as we went. Our arses looking like pincushions, we sprinted for the comparative safety of a nearby forest. The brownies chased us a long way into it before at last giving up. Now well and truly lost, we decided to stop for a while and pull the arrows out of each other.

Now, it is a little known fact that brownies dip their arrows in the sperm of the green tree frog. This evil poison acts fatally on kittens, but has a merely hallucinogenic effect on anything larger than your average moggy. Not that any of us knew this at the time. Actually, the first I knew about it, I was sitting there pulling arrows out of Boglith's arse, when a very surprised-looking dwarf floated past me. I was just about to say something, but Boglith's bum told me it wasn't such a good idea. As I was about to argue, Boglith himself began crawling towards the stool, saying, 'Hello ... you know, you're the only one who understands me.'

It wasn't too long before the moaning and banging began, not that I could hear it over Knobby's rendition of, 'Gold, Gold, Gold', or Gilbert trying to turn his hat into a woman. For some strange reason, just before I slipped into unconsciousness, I was starting to find Knobby very attractive. Apparently, green frog sperm is also a powerful aphrodisiac.

Next day when I finally came round, some time in the late afternoon, I was more than a little worried to find myself naked, and with a scary-looking rash. I had woken up hugging the stool to my chest. Worse still, I had a mouthful of pubic hair, and I wasn't about to ask whose the hell it was. We all got dressed in rather a hurry, as none of us seemed to be wearing clothes, never taking our eyes off the floor.

'Now what?' I asked, trying my best not to look at the stool, which I could swear was smiling at me.

'We could always go back to the village. I mean, we did kill the dragon,' Knobby smiled.

'Almost,' I said, trying to fish the last few hairs out of my mouth.

'They don't know that,' put in a sheepish Boglith.

'What about those brownies? I don't want to go through another night like last night,' I said.

'What about last night?' Gilbert asked.

'Oh, nothing.'

'Anyway, brownies never go into villages,' he lied.

'Unless they're looking for someone,' Boglith added.

'You mean like us?'

'It's the getting to the village that worries me,' I grumbled.

'Look, when we get there we'll be heroes!' Gil smiled.

'OK, I'm with you,' I decided, thinking of village girls and cleavages you could ski down.

It was about this point my concerns began to turn to panic, for when we moved off, the stool began to follow me.

9

The Curse

The forest seemed to grow thick and dark in every direction; large branches hung heavy with moss and lichen, blanking out all but the merest light from above. With no path to guide us, we just started walking in the first direction our fancy took us (which turned out to be the wrong one, as it happened). The wet earth and thick undergrowth made it slow going. In parts we were forced to hack our way through the deepening wood.

'Does anyone else think we're going the wrong way?' Knobby asked, hacking at a vine with his axe.

'Yes!' I answered, pulling another vine from my hair.

'Oh good ... Just thought I'd ask.'

That night, having made little progress, we decided to make camp and try again in the morning. The damp forest made lighting a fire impossible, even with Gilbert's help, so we just huddled together for warmth in the eerie darkness.

'We're going to die, aren't we?' Boglith asked, as the forest seemed to come alive with the dark, and the air was filled with the sounds of the night.

'Oh yeah.'

'Probably.'

'No doubt.' I tried to smile.

'Thanks, I feel a lot better now,' Boglith muttered.

Next morning, having slept in a bramble bush, the harsh

light of dawn gave us no joy, as we once again began our long toil through the dense thicket. It was fast approaching dusk when we stumbled, at last, upon a path. It was dark and lonely; pale mist seemed to shroud it and the smell of death hung heavy in the air, but, it was a lifeline, a way out of the accursed forest, and to freedom. It also meant I could stop and pull the thorns out of my bloody arse.

'We're saved!' Knobby winced as he pulled a thorn from his own backside.

'I vote we make camp here,' Boglith suggested.

'Why?' I asked.

'Because we're here,' he answered, slumping to the floor.

As we made camp by the side of the road the moon slowly rose, and the night air came alive with the cry of the wolf.

'Er, I don't want to worry anyone, but that's a full moon,' Gil said, pointing up.

'So?'

'Full moon ... wolves – any of that ring a bell?' the wizard snapped.

'Nope.'

'Werewolves.'

'Oh, what is a werewolf?' I asked.

'It's a man that turns into a wolf with every full moon.'

'Oh. Why does he do that, then?' I smiled, dumbly.

'It's a curse,' he explained.

'Oh, that would be fantastic to be able to do that,' I laughed.

'Oh, come on,' Knobby grinned, 'you're barking up the wrong tree if you think we believe that.'

'Look, they're real and they're nasty, and they like hurting people,' Gilbert snapped.

'What, so you think we should keep watch?' Knobby asked, clutching his axe and casting nervous glances around.

'No, I think we should just all go to sleep and get eaten alive.'

'Er?'

'Well, let's just think about it for a minute, shall we?' Gilbert shouted, 'first we all ran away from a rampaging cow...'

'Demon cow,' Knobby corrected.

'OK,' Gilbert sighed, 'demon cow. Then we walk, open-eyed, right into a troll's cave. Then of course we had great fun in the dragon's lair, not to mention what happened to poor Lud. From there we all strolled right into the heart of kitten heaven.'

'So what's your point?' I asked.

'Let's just say we are not the luckiest adventurers in the realm ... and the last thing I want right now is to be a werewolf's lunch!' he snapped.

'Oh, OK then, we'll keep watch,' I said.

'Knobby can take the first watch,' Boglith smiled.

'Why me?' Knobby stormed.

'Because it was your idea.'

'Look, just wake us if we're all going to die horribly,' Gilbert pleaded.

We settled down to sleep, Knobby clutched his axe and the mist around us began to thicken and swirl as if creeping towards its unsuspecting victims.

...Twelve naked nubile young Valkyries were slowly massaging oil into every part of my naked body. They had just begun to reach my groin and massage inwards when a scream rent the air. The dream vanished in a puff of consciousness and I was awake. Knobby's girl-like screams filled the still forest air. I scrambled to my feet, grabbing what I thought was my weapon, only to find myself standing there waving the stool around by its weapon. Dropping the stool's wooden wand, I hastily groped around for my real sword. Running over to Knobby, I was just in time to see him tear an extremely fluffy, bright pink rabbit from his face and throw it to the earth. Unperturbed, the rampant rabbit bounced back on down the path.

'Little git!' shouted Knobby, touching his blood-soaked face. 'That sod just leapt out of that tree at me,' he continued clutching his axe.

'That must have been hare-raising!' Gilbert said. 'Who's for rabbit stew?'

At the sound of our voices the bouncing bunny turned to stare at us.

'Come here, little rabbit, come to nice uncle Knobby ... I only want to chop off your head and eat you!' Knobby cooed.

As the four of us stood there, stomachs tight and weapons at the ready, with the bunny bouncing towards us, we saw to our horror that this was no ordinary bright pink rabbit. With each passing bong it began to change. On the first bounce it began to grow, with the second talons sprouted, then teeth. On the fourth bunny bong it began to stand erect, so by the time it was upon us we were faced with a very large, angry, six-foot, bright pink rabbit. With a blast of rancid carrot breath, the monstrous apparition spoke.

'GO AWAY!' it bellowed.

'OK.'

'Sure.'

'No problem.'

'We'll just be going, then,' I said, edging away.

We slowly backed away, the wererabbit turned and hopped into the mist, and as its fluffy white tail vanished, Knobby spoke.

'That'll be me shafted, then.'

'What are you talking about?'

'This,' Knobby said, pointing to his face.

'What? I know you're ugly, but what?'
'Tell them, Gilbert.'
'He's right. He's been bitten, and the curse passed on. Next full moon he will change; he will become a creature of the night, a wererabbit.' Gilbert giggled.

After a great deal of agonizing soul-searching, I came up with something I thought might help. 'Sorry, mate,' I said, slapping him on the back.

'Sorry? You're bloody sorry? Well, that's all right then. I've been cursed to walk this earth as a werebunny to the end of my days and you're sorry. I'm going to grow big fluffy ears, a small white tail and have one hell of a sodding carrot fetish, but that's OK because you're flaming sorry.'

'Look, just calm down,' I said. 'Look on the bright side. You might get lucky ... I mean, rabbits are always at it.'

'Yeah, but, with other bloody rabbits. Thanks a lot, that makes me feel so much better.'

'Calm down ... just calm down!' Gilbert shouted.

'We simply get a witch to remove your curse.'

'Where are we going to find a witch round here?'

A dry cackle echoed through the trees, as if the forest was laughing at us. Knobby shivered.

'The wind. Anyway,' Gilbert continued, 'we'll find one in the next village we come across.'

'We'd better, because if not, I'll...' a slow, moronic grin spread over Knobby's face, his eyes took on a glazed look, and he fell face first into the dirt. Boglith could be seen standing just behind him, holding a small brownie arrow in his hand. 'Thought it might come in handy,' he smiled.

'Where did you get that?' I asked.

'Pulled it out of your arse!'

We dragged the lifeless form of Knobby to the side of the road and settled down to make camp once again.

'What now?' I asked.

'We just have to get Stumpy here to a village with a witch before the next full moon,' Gilbert answered.

'You lot try and get some sleep. I'll take the first watch, just in case old Thumper comes back,' I said.

As the others settled down to sleep, that same dry crackle echoed through the darkness again. My thoughts turned to all our ill-fated adventures since leaving home. Had it all been worth it, just for a few free drinks? As I thought about it I had to admit, no, it bloody wasn't, but then I had been sober for far too long now. As Gilbert took the second watch, my thoughts turned to a large bowl of rabbit stew, and once again I thought of Knobby on a spit.

The days passed and we had no success in our search for a village. Then disaster struck again; as we were passing under the eaves of a giant oak, a huge black stallion sprang from the shadows as if from nowhere.

Rearing high in front of us, we could just make out a small, black-cloaked figure holding on for dear life. Dressed from head to toe in black velvet, the masked stranger spoke:

'Stand and deliver!' he panted, pointing a small crossbow at us.

'Do we look like pizza delivery boys to you?' I asked.

'Deliver what?' Boglith asked, spreading his arms.

'Your money or your life!'

'How's that work, then?' Knobby asked.

'You give me your money and I won't kill you. I am a highwayman, you know.'

'Sounds fair, but we're on a path,' Knobby pointed out.

'All right, all right,' he sighed, 'I'm a bloody pathman.'

'So what's a pathman then?' I asked.

'It's the same as a highwayman, but on a path, OK?'

'So what's a highwayman then?' I asked.

'Now look, you prat, it's a robber. Now hand over your gold,' the small man answered.

'You get much passing trade out on a deserted path, in the middle of nowhere?' Boglith asked.

'Well, now that I come to think about it, no.'

'So why don't you try somewhere else?' I asked.

'By the time I'd managed to save up enough money for the cloak, all the good roads had gone.'

'You're a thief. Why should you care if there's another highwayman there?' I asked.

'True, but all the other highwaymen are bigger than me.'

'So why do it, then? You could always try something else,' Boglith pointed out helpfully.

'Well, I've got the cloak now, so I might as well give it a try. So if you could, please hand over all your coins.'

'But we haven't got any coins,' I lied.

'OK boys, now let's cut the shit. Just give me all your gold or I'll kill the ugly one,' he snapped, aiming his crossbow at Knobby.

'And why would that be a bad thing?' I asked.

'Just give him the gold. I'm in no mood for this,' Knobby snorted through gritted teeth, his hand curling round his axe haft.

'All right, all right, take them,' I sighed, tossing him the small bag of coins we'd found in the dragon's lair.

'Is this it? Hardly seems worth the effort.'

'Of course that's it, what the hell do you expect? I mean, here we are, out in the middle of God knows where; of course we're going to be carrying tons of bags of gold around, you pillock!' I snapped.

'Ah well, pleasure doing business with you gentlemen,' he smiled, pocketing the coins. 'No one's ever let me rob them before.'

'That figures,' groaned Boglith.

With a shout and a flourish of his hat, our wayward

robber reared his stallion, and promptly fell off. Now that I come to think of it, this would have been the perfect opportunity to jump our would-be robber and get our gold back but, of course, we didn't, we just watched him climb back on his horse and ride away.

As we continued on the trail things did not improve.
'This is turning out to be a real shitty day,' Knobby muttered, one dank morning.
'Could be worse,' Gilbert said.
'It is worse,' Boglith sighed, pointing up the path. 'Look.'
There up ahead lay a fork in the path.
'Oh, fork,' Gilbert sighed.
'Which way do we go?' I asked.
'How the hell do I know?' Boglith whined.
'There's a very simple way to find out,' said Gilbert. 'Knobby, which way would you go?'
'Left,' Knobby answered without hesitation.
'Then we go right,' Gilbert beamed.
'What?'
'With the luck he's having, I wouldn't let him choose from a bloody drinks menu,' he said, pointing at the dwarf.
'OK, right it is,' I said, starting down the path.
'Er, right's the other way.' Gilbert tapped me on the shoulder.
'I knew that,' I said, starting down the right-hand path, 'I was just testing.'
We trudged along the path for all that day without seeing another soul or any signs of life, and as the day began to draw to a close, Gilbert was forced to admit his mistake.
'Maybe we should have gone left after all.' He sighed.

10

The Witch

As the night of the next full moon approached, the strain began to get to the dwarf. His face began to twitch and his nerves to fray.

'Look, I don't think we're going to find a village before sundown tonight,' Gilbert said, as the sun went down.

'That'll be me screwed, then,' Knobby snapped, his temper flaring.

'So what are we going to do...'

'ARRRGHHH!' Knobby's chilling scream filled the forest air. Spinning round I was in time to see Knobby fall to his knees, a fresh scream on his lips. With another heart-rending howl he fell forward on to his hands and knees, then began to rip and tear at his clothes. Small tufts of pink fur began to sprout all over his shrinking form. Falling on to his back, his whole body started to convulse and shake; white froth and drool sprayed from his screaming mouth. His teeth and ears began to grow as his dick started to shrink. With a blood-curdling scream his back seemed to arch to breaking point. Large muscles swelled and grew on his legs, which seemed to stretch, then with a loud crack that brought tears to my eyes, folded in on themselves. With a final shriek the convulsions began to subside, leaving us with an unconscious, bright pink bunny.

'What now?' I whispered, drawing my sword and edging

away. At the sound of my voice the rabbit's eyes snapped open and his terrified cries filled the air.

'Knobby?' Boglith asked.

'You all right, mate?' I asked, waving my sword in his general direction.

'I think so,' he said, looking around. 'How do I look?' he asked, staring at his paws and wiggling his nose.

'Good.'

'You look fine,' Boglith said.

'Really?'

'No ... Sorry mate, you look bloody awful!' Boglith smiled.

'It's not that bad re...'

'ARRRGHHH!' Knobby's shriek blocked out Boglith's voice. 'Where's my bloody dick gone?'

'I'm sure it's still there ... somewhere.' I looked vaguely at his crotch.

'Don't worry, it'll be back in the morning,' Gilbert smiled.

'What woman's going to want me with a knob this small?'

'You're a pink rabbit. Your wand size is the least of your problems right now.'

'Here mate, have a drink,' I said, offering him some home-made brew.

'How am I going to drink that? In case you hadn't noticed, I'm a bloody bunny!'

'I know you must be hopping mad,' I laughed.

'That's it! Come here so I can bite you on the ankle.'

There was a loud crash, and Knobby was cut short as Boglith bounced the stool across the back of his head.

'Come on, let's prop him against this tree,' Boglith said, dragging the unconscious rabbit to a nearby tree. 'Now let's try and get some sleep. We can deal with Big-Ears in the morning.'

'I bet you've just been dying to call him that,' I said.

The night passed peacefully, as we slept huddled together against the now surprisingly comfortable dwarf.

Next morning the restored form of Knobby still lay slumped against the tree where we had left him.

'You all right, mate?' I asked, shaking the dwarf awake.

Awaking with a start, Knobby's hand flew down in a panic. Grabbing his wand a slow smile spread across his face.

'Yeah, I'm fine,' he smiled, not letting go.

As Knobby got himself dressed (always a tricky manoeuvre whilst holding on to your dick), the rest of us went in search of something to eat. Being the true woodsmen we all were, we didn't find a thing, so once Knobby had got his trousers on, it was back to the trail.

Another thing the minstrels always forget to sing about is how flaming dull life really is on the trail. I mean, think about it, what the hell is there for you to do? You can look at the trees ... or you can look at the trees. If you're really lucky, you might just see a tree.

As the long day wore relentlessly on, the sun continued its onslaught. By noon the temperature was almost unbearable.

'Greetings, weary travellers,' a voice said. Turning round we came face to face with three of the most beautiful women I had ever seen. They were dressed in little more than two strips of tanned leather, that left little to the imagination. My jaw hit the floor almost as fast as my dick hit my chin. Their easy smiles and colossal cleavages completely took my mind away from my empty stomach.

'My name is Natasha. You have travelled far, and are in need of rest,' said the first, in honeyed tones.

'Come, let us worship you with our bodies,' said the second.

'Yes, come and make love to us all!' said the first.

'We have been alone for too long. Come play with us,' their silky voices purred, as they slowly slid their hands up their thighs.

'Oh,' I said, limping forward.

No sooner had we moved towards the women, our arms and tongues sticking out, when Gilbert jumped in front of us, barring our path.

'Stop!' he screamed.

'What?'

'Get the hell out of the way,' Knobby snapped.

'Wait! Can't you see it?'

'Of course I can see it. They're making my eyes hurt,' I drooled.

'No look ... they're just mirages caused by the heat,' Gilbert snapped.

'All I can see is three pair of beautiful tits that are just dying to have my head put between them and jiggled about a bit!'

'No, they have a strange aura about them.'

'Yes, it's called being horny. It doesn't happen around us too often.'

'No, look, trust me. Something's not right. Just ignore them and let's go,' Gilbert said.

'But I don't want to,' I moaned.

'They're not real,' Gilbert snarled.

'They look real.'

'Well, they're not.'

'Let me have a quick feel to make sure,' I said, moving towards the ladies with arms outstretched.

'No,' Gilbert snapped, pulling me backwards.

'But just look at those cleavages,' Boglith moaned.

'Just close your eyes and come on.'

With a sigh, I closed my eyes and slowly limped after the wizard. I hadn't gone but a few steps, when I heard Knobby's horny grunts. Spinning round I could see both

Knobby and the stool advancing on the women, with tongues (and legs in the case of the stool), outstretched.

'Oy, you leave those imaginary women alone,' I screamed.

With a long sigh and one last longing look, the pair of them followed on behind us.

'Why does this always happen to us?' Natasha moaned, stamping her feet in anger.

'I know. That's the second time this week men have walked right past us, and to think I wore my best bra for this!'

'What? Best bra means more cleavage!'

'Of course. Anyway, this is all your fault.'

'How the hell can this be my fault?'

'I told you to have your hair done.'

'My roots are fine.'

'Not from this angle, darling.'

'Oh, that's nice, coming from the split end queen over here.'

'You bitch!'

As we slowly limped away, our hearts heavy, the faint sounds of large-breasted women trying to pull each other's hair out echoed through the still forest air behind us.

The oppressing heat slowly began to fade with the hazy light of evening, leaving behind only the promise of rain. With the excitement of the mirages little more than a fading memory, I was becoming acutely aware of how empty my stomach was. As the pale light of twilight began to fade, the last rays of light revealed a small, tumbledown little hut away in the distance. Even this far away we could see the smoking chimney.

'Looks like someone's at home.'

'Maybe they'll be kind and give us some food,' Knobby said, doubling his pace towards the cabin.

'With our luck it's probably a banshee's summer home,' I moaned, falling into step behind the others.

'And you just know she's going to be pleased to see us.'

As we approached the hut the door swung open with an eerie creak. We stood there, fully prepared to run away, while a small, rickety old woman slowly emerged. Dressed in little more than a few filthy rags, her dirty hair hung long, in greasy, lank rat's tails. This strange old woman had witch written all over her – well, actually, she had it written on a large sign which she propped up outside the door. Sitting down on a small stool, she spoke.

'At last the travellers come. You have come far ... There, sit down, take your rest.' She beckoned.

'Bloody hell,' I gasped, 'someone that's actually pleased to see us!'

As we gratefully slumped to the ground, she turned to each of us and fixed us with an icy gaze. Then, with a cruel smile, she turned on Boglith.

'First the elf. Your past is full of great pain and bitterness. You have walked too long hand in hand with disaster and sorrow. You have suffered more years than you wish to remember. All this you know, but it makes me feel better to rub it in. You are a sad, lonely man, with little or no joy left in life to him.'

'Thanks very much.'

'Don't interrupt. You learn nothing while your lips flap!'

'Sorry.'

'I said shut up, boy!' she snapped. 'Now listen. Trouble will hunt and haunt your every step. You will try to run and hide, but she draws ever closer with each passing second.'

Boglith's face turned ashen white.

'Your fear of women will bring you to your knees... To put it simply, elf, you're more than a little screwed. And you!' she snapped, fixing me with an evil gaze, 'stop bleeding describing what's going on while I'm talking, and you, yes you, reading this story, sit up straight while you read this bit.'

She then transferred her evil gaze to Gilbert.

'Next, I come to you, wizard. Your wand is your biggest problem. It has led you from one orifice to another, with never a thought between. You are a man of decaying moral fibre. You have spent your whole perverted existence in the pointless pursuit of meaningless carnal pleasures, and what has it got you, apart from the clap?'

'Laid!' Gilbert answered, with a wry smile.

'That wasn't a question, child!' she snapped. 'Now listen to me. Your pitiful life as a wizard was short-lived at best. Once again, your insatiable appetites got the better of you.'

'I slept with the head wizard's wife ... and mother-in-law ... and goat, now I come to think about it,' Gilbert said proudly.

'What happened?' I asked.

'I got a life in exile, and a really painful skin rash.' He explained.

'What did he do to his wife?' Knobby asked.

'He turned her into that cat you ate, and you don't want to know what he did to his mother-in-law,' he said.

'What about the goat?'

'For some reason he didn't seem to feel the goat's betrayal quite so badly.'

'Have you lot quite finished?' the witch snapped. 'There is little I can tell you about your future. The paths of wizards, even failed wizards, are always misty at best. All I may tell you is this: your destiny approaches faster than you can imagine. Look to your best feature to guide your path. Oh, and by the way, my bedroom door will be unlocked tonight,' she said with a wink.

Then it was my turn. My stomach churned, as she turned her evil gaze on me.

'Now I come to you,' she said, her voice as welcoming

as the grave. A slow, cruel smile spread across her weathered face, sending shivers down my spine. 'I have looked forward to meeting you for many years now. But now at last, I may tell you little. Your past is unknown to all but me, and I am not going to tell you. You are an utter failure as a man; your great personal cowardice and small amount of charm have done little but push you from one bottle to another. You have worked hard to become what you are now, and you have forgotten who or what you are, but if the gods are with you (which they aren't), you may discover the truth behind your past and uncover your heart's desire. What I will tell you is this, your quest now stands at a crossroads ... so choose carefully.'

'Is that it?'

'Yes.'

'Wow, I thought you people only ever give bad news,' I said.

'Is that what you want to hear?'

'No.'

'So who or what is he, then?' Knobby interrupted.

'I am not going to tell you that!' she snapped.

'Shut up, or she'll probably tell me my knob's going to fall off,' I said, slapping him across the back of his head.

'Last, I come to you of the little people, travelling under a curse. Although, I am forced to admit, I didn't expect you to be such an ugly bastard. For you I have no future or past to read; for you I have only a simple bargain: in return for one whole night of passion, I will remove your curse for ever.'

'That's it, one bang-bang, no bunny-bunny?'

'That's all. One night of pleasure for your freedom,' she smiled, revealing a mouth full of black, rotting teeth.

'What are we waiting for then?' Knobby grinned, climbing to his feet.

'You're sure about this, mate?' I asked, grabbing him by the arm.

'What?'
'Well, she's not exactly...'
'Not exactly what?'
'Well ... human.'
'Hey, any port in a storm,' he smiled, 'and I'd do anything not to have my dick shrink again.'
'You put it in there, it might fall off!' I said.
'Wait here a minute,' she said, disappearing back into her cabin. Some minutes later she emerged carrying a large platter of black bread and cheese, and a large paper bag.
'What's that for?' Knobby asked, pointing to the bag.
'It's for you.'
'What?'
'You put it over your head to cover your face, you ugly git!'
'Oh!'
'This is for you,' she said, handing me the food. 'Now, come on.' She grabbed Knobby's arm and dragged him into the cabin.

As the door slammed shut we began to devour the food.
'Oh my God, will you look at the size of that!' echoed from the cabin.

Before long the cabin began to shake and the moaning and groaning started. In even less time it had finished.
'That was bloody quick,' I said.
'Knobby's always been a little short.'

Within the space of another few seconds the snoring began. With the last rays of light the rest of us bedded down for the night.

As the first rays of dawn crested the forest roof, Knobby's bare arse flew out of the cabin window, followed by a bright blue flame.
'What the bloody hell's wrong with you ... petal?' Knobby asked, from a crumpled heap on the floor.
'What's hell's wrong? Five minutes, five bleeding minutes.

I've had sheep last longer than that!' she roared, her face flushed with fury.

'I was tired,' Knobby stammered, pulling up his trousers.

'The bargain, now I come to think about it, was for one night of carnal passion, not five flaming minutes.'

'Well, you know how it is. I was nervous.'

'Nervous! No more excuses, you gutless worm. Your pitiful performance has sealed your fate for ever. No longer will you be cursed to walk the earth as a lowly wererabbit, no, nothing so grandiose for you. You are cursed anew. You will be forced to wander the land as the lowliest of all creatures. I curse you to spend the rest of your miserable existence as a lowly weretortoise!'

With that she threw up her arms and, with a flash of blue light, Knobby was instantly engulfed in a large puff of blue smoke and flame.

'As for the rest of you, I'll leave you with these few words of warning: Beware being idle in March.'

'What?'

'I don't know. I read it in a book, somewhere. Now bugger off, the lot of you!'

With that there was a loud clap of thunder and a puff of smoke. As the smoke slowly swirled and cleared, the witch just stood there, looking, it has to be said, rather perplexed.

'Bollocks. I've never got that to work!' she snapped. 'Just piss off!' she screamed, storming into the hut and slamming the door behind her.

'Bitch, I'll kill her,' Knobby yelled, scrambling for his axe.

'Aren't you in enough shit already?' I asked.

'Yeah, you don't want to piss her off even more,' Boglith said.

'Look, come on, we'll get it sorted out at the next village,' Gil said.

'That's what you said last time, and hasn't that turned out just dandy?' Knobby sneered.

'Come on, best make a move,' Boglith said, starting off down the trail.

It stretched along all day without the merest hint of any village, or any living soul. To make matters worse, with the fading light of day, the long-promised rain arrived with a vengeance. Taking shelter in the forest, we made camp for the night. Not that it helped. Within a few short minutes we were soaked to the bone. The rain continued unabated long into the night. By the first light of morning, the downpour had turned to a flood. 'That'll be us wet, then,' Knobby said, stepping out into the downpour.

We sloshed along most of that day, the rain getting heavier with each step. At one point the trail became completely impassable, forcing us to take shelter under another tree, until the rain showed at least some slight sign of stopping. For almost an hour we sat, huddled together under the branches, waiting for the infernal rain to stop.

'I think it might be stopping,' Knobby said, waving his hand outside the tree.

'Still spitting,' Boglith said.

'No, I'm not,' Knobby snapped.

'Trail still looks a lot wet,' Boglith said, as Knobby stepped out from beneath the tree and promptly disappeared with a big splash.

'You all right, mate?' I asked, as we dragged the coughing and spluttering dwarf out of the large hole he seemed to have found himself in.

'That'll be my bath early,' Knobby gasped between coughs.

'Er, guys,' said Gil, who was still standing under the tree, 'look.' He was pointing to the hole.

'Yes, it's a bloody hole,' Knobby croaked.

'No, look.'

Once again under the tree we could clearly see what the wizard was pointing at. The large hole Knobby had fallen into bore a striking resemblance to a giant footprint.

'Oh shit. That'll be us dead again, then!' Knobby gasped, casting nervous glances around.

'No problem,' Gilbert smiled. 'There's a very simple way to deal with any giant we may meet.'

'What?' I asked.

'Run!' he shouted as once again his arse disappeared down the trail.

It was some minutes later that exhaustion overcame us, forcing us to stop and rest. As I knelt by the side of the trail, gasping for breath, I saw through a break in the trees the entrance to a small cave. No sooner had I pointed it out to the others, than Knobby's anger flared again.

'You've got to be kidding,' he snapped. 'There's no way you're getting my arse into another bloody cave.'

'Why not?' I asked. 'At least we'd be out of this rain.'

'Oh yeah, and if we're really lucky, this one won't be full of brownies, trolls or flaming dragons. No, forget it, there's just no way.'

'OK, OK. We'll just keep walking in the bleeding rain then,' I snapped, and with that I climbed to my feet and set off down the trail. It was approaching dusk when we finally drew towards the outskirts of the forest.

11

Geraldine

On the outskirts of the forest was a small rundown village, surrounding the pillars of a ruined castle. Many of the houses were in an advanced state of decay; fields had been left untilled, the streets were deserted.

'Ah, fresh air,' Gilbert said, sniffing the air.

'At least we're out of that accursed forest,' I said.

'And at least we can find somewhere out of the rain,' Knobby chipped in, running for the cover of the nearest building with half a roof.

The village seemed to have a strange, eerie feel about it. For one thing, the rain stopped almost the second we entered it, almost as if it had been driving us there. The village had obviously long since been deserted, but I couldn't rid myself of the feeling of being watched. It had been deserted in a hurry too, as carts and market stalls were left overturned in the main square.

'Something strange is going on here,' said Boglith, as we walked through the streets.

'I know. Where are all the people?' I asked, looking around.

'Plague?' Gilbert suggested.

'That, or one big monster,' I added, thoughtfully.

'Oh, isn't that just lovely,' Knobby snapped, 'I've only got twenty-five days left before I turn into a sodding weretortoise, but that's OK, because in the meantime I'm either going to catch the plague and die, or be eaten alive by some big horrible thing. Now isn't that a perfect end to a truly shitty day?'

'If it was the plague, where are all the bodies?' Boglith asked.

'Eaten probably,' Gil thought out loud.

'Yeah, by the big horrible thing,' Knobby said.

'Let's just dry out and get some sleep. If we're lucky there may be something to eat around here,' Gil said.

'You mean apart from us, that is?' Knobby replied, with a hollow laugh.

'Look, we'll be gone in the morning, let's just get warm and try and get some sleep,' I pleaded.

We took shelter in the nearest dry hut and lit a fire. As I started to wring the water out of my loincloth, the voices began.

'Get out, save yourself,' seemed to be whispered in the very wind. Spinning round to see if the others were taking the piss, all I could see was Knobby drying his enormous dick by the firelight. (At least I hope that is what he was doing.) The rest of them were just huddled around the small fire, trying to dry out their own underwear. I must have imagined the whole thing; not enough beer and no food was playing tricks with my very small mind; I just settled down to sleep, with three wet naked men. Believe me, I never opened my eyes all night. That night my dreams were filled with scenes of pain and terror. It was worse than a night on Knobby's revolting home-brew. I awoke with a start the next morning, the beginning of a scream on my lips.

Staggering to my feet, the whole room was full of a translucent white mist. It seemed to come from all around and cover the room like a cloak.

'You farted again, Knobby?' I asked, shaking him awake with the toe of my boot, moving outside.

The mist was everywhere; it shrouded the whole village, cloaking it in a veil of white.

Almost as soon as I stepped from the hut, the music began. It was soft and sweet; it seemed to intoxicate the senses and soothe the soul. This heavenly music seemed to come from everywhere, slowly it drew me towards the round castle, like the caress of a gentle lover. My feet seemed to follow the music of their own volition, and I was drawn towards the ruins as if led by the very soul.

'What in God's name is that bloody awful noise?' Knobby shouted.

Looking down I could just about see the dwarf, as if through a haze. Knobby was standing in front of me holding his ears, as if in terrible pain. As suddenly as it began the music vanished, leaving me with a strange sense of loneliness and sorrow, that weighed heavily on my soul.

'I vote we run away,' Knobby suggested. 'Terribly fast,' he added.

'I've got to find that music,' I said.

'What! Are you out of your tiny mind?' Knobby shouted at me. 'Is there anything in there?' he ranted, knocking me on the head.

'Oh come on, how can it hurt to have a quick look round?' Gilbert said, walking up beside me.

'Er, hello, did everyone's IQ just drop when I wasn't looking? It's *us*, of course it can bloody hurt!' he stormed, shaking his head.

'Oh, come on,' I said, 'just one look around, then we'll go, I promise.'

We started off towards the ruins, but the stool seemed a little reluctant to follow.

'You see,' Knobby shouted, 'even the stool doesn't want to go.'

'Oh you're right – we must take the advice of a magical wooden stool... Come on, we'll only be five minutes.'

'That'll be you all insane, then,' Knobby shouted.

The nearer we drew to the entrance of the ruins, the thicker the mist seemed to become, until it seemed we were almost wading through a river of mist. At the broken-down gates to the castle were some of the most exquisitely beautiful statues I had ever seen; life-size carvings of men in every possible pose. As we made our way deeper into the ruins we came across more and more of the beautiful, but strangely worrying carvings. It was as if some mad sculptor had gone to work, creating havoc before anyone could stop him. The deeper we went into the strange mist, the more statues we encountered; knights in armour, men with weapons drawn ... but no women.

'I wonder why no women?' Boglith asked.

'Don't know. Maybe the sculptor was gay,' I answered.

The sculptures were everywhere now, forcing us to climb over them at points.

'Can any sane person tell me what the bloody hell we're doing here, and not running away, like normal people?' Knobby demanded, as we climbed over the fallen statue of a knight. 'I think it's long past time to go.' He jumped down from the knight's groin. There was a loud squelching noise from under Knobby's feet, as they met the floor.

'What the bleeding hell have I just stepped in?' he asked, looking at the bottom of his boots with a grimace.

As we all peered through the mist, we saw what seemed to be what was left of one extremely dead, half-eaten knight.

'Is it me, or does that look like the same knight that was in the bar that night?' I asked, poking the remains with my boot.

'Well the bastard won't be getting any free drinks this time,' Gilbert laughed.

'Amusing as all this is, can we please get the hell out of this nightmare?' Knobby asked.

'Too right,' Boglith said, backing slowly down the passage. We hadn't gone more than a few steps when Boglith stopped dead in his tracks.

'Hang on a minute. I've heard those monster stories the minstrels tell around the fire late at night. The victims always back into the monster.'

'So?' I asked.

'So let's walk on and avoid getting more than a little dead, like our friend over there,' he said, pointing to the knight's body.

'But that's the way out,' Gilbert protested.

'That's why the monster will be waiting for us there.'

'What, outside?' I asked.

'Yes.'

'Where we've just come from?'

'Yes.'

'Hang on ... let me get this straight. You're saying let's walk right into the monster's lair to avoid it?' I gasped.

'Look, every time we run away it goes horribly wrong, right?'

'Right.'

'So what else can go wrong?'

'We could die,' I said, as the elf started back down the passage.

'That'll be us dead, then,' Knobby whispered, following along behind him.

We had been going for less than a minute, when once again Boglith stopped us.

'Wait a minute,' he said. 'In those stories it's always the poor sod in the front that gets it first. Why am I at the front?'

'We're trying to tell you something,' Gilbert said.

'I always thought it was the bloke at the rear that got it first,' Knobby said, 'and hang on a minute ... that's me!'

'All right, you take the front then. That way if I'm right you'll die first.' Boglith smiled.

So off we went again, but for some strange reason I ended up taking the lead. We hadn't gone too much further when the smell hit us. It was the unmistakable smell of death. It was at about this point my feet decided my brain had gone out to lunch, and started backing me down the passage.

'Oh for the love of Satan, will you just come bloody in,' a voice echoed down the corridor.

It was only then that I noticed the eyes; two flame-red, evil eyes stared at us from the darkness. A scream broke through the silence as Gilbert jumped forward, casting yet another spell. In the confusion that followed, not to mention blind terror, he must have cast the wrong spell; a small blue spark flew from the silver ring on his finger into the darkness. As for the rest of us, we had hit the safety of the floor, knowing Gilbert's aim all too well. As I looked up from my hiding place I could just make out the still form of the wizard staring at his hands, no doubt wondering where his fireball had got to.

Suddenly, a large Medusa issued forth from the darkness, the snakes on her head hissing and spitting as she came. But as she approached, no stony gaze petrified her victims; she just charged at Gilbert, her arms outstretched, hissing: 'Oh baby, come to momma.'

Before any of us could react she leapt forward, grabbing the now doomed Gilbert by the ankle, and dragged him back to her lair. The last thing we saw was poor Gilbert, kicking and screaming, trying desperately to claw his way out of her deadly grasp. Slowly, she dragged him inch by inch into the enveloping darkness. The noises that followed would have turned an elephant's stomach. Screams of pure pain and pleasure emanated from the lair, mixed with the odd cry of 'HELP ME!'

'That'll be him screwed, then,' Knobby said.

'So, what do we do now?' Boglith asked, staring into the darkness.

'Only one thing to do.'
'What?'
'Run!' I shouted.

Now it is said that a true and honest hero will never stand idly by and let another human being suffer but, thank the gods, I am not a true and honest hero, so I did a runner, like the true and honest coward I am. As I spun round to make my escape, I tripped over the ever-present stool which, as always, was standing right behind me. As my face smashed into the cold stone floor, my forehead met a tiny ring of cold, golden metal; not that I noticed at the time. I just staggered to my feet and stumbled on, the ring now safely embedded in my skull. As we scrambled blinking into the light at the end of the passage, something seemed out of place. It took a few minutes for the full reality to sink in.

'The village's gone!' Knobby gasped.

He was right. Not one signpost or shack was to be seen. The whole village had vanished. But what was there was a dark and menacing shadow, which slowly began to encroach on the entrance to the ruins ... and us. It seemed to crowd in from all directions, covering everything in a cloak of darkness, blocking out the sun as it came.

'Oh shit,' Boglith moaned.

Time seemed to stand still as we stared at the invading shadow with mounting despair. A slow, slithering noise made me spin round in terror, fearing I was the Medusa's next hapless victim. The sight that met my eyes will haunt my nightmares for ever. The Medusa came slithering from the shadows, carrying the half-naked form of Gilbert in her arms; but once again no stony gaze issued forth.

'I think I broke him.' She smiled sweetly, or as sweetly as a half-snake, half-woman, with a face like the back end of a pig, can do.

Gilbert turned his head to face us and, lighting a cigarette said:

'Hi guys, this is Geraldine.'
'Er...'
'Ah...'
'Hello,' I stuttered. I mean, what do you say to a Medusa called Geraldine, who's just screwed your friend half to death? So we stood there, staring at our feet, until it dawned on me that Geraldine was staring at me.
'Are you staring at me?' I asked, trembling.
'Oh, sorry.'
'Er ... no, aren't I suppose to turn to stone or something?'
'Oh no, we can only do that before we lose our virginity,' she smiled, 'and Gillypoos has just taken care of that!'
'Oh ... so why are you staring at me?'
'It's just that I see you found my ring,' she smiled, pointing to my head.
As I wiped the blood away from my face, I felt the small ring embedded in my forehead. It took about five minutes, and Knobby's dagger, to lever the thing loose. In the end I was left holding a tiny ring of golden metal, and more than a little of my skin and blood.
'Here ... sorry about that,' I said, offering her the mess.
'No, no, you keep it. I've got all I want right here,' she said, hugging Gilbert to her breast (and it has to said it was quite a nice chest). 'At long last I know how it feels to be a real woman ... and boy, it feels good!' she finished with a shiver.
'Thanks, but it'll never fit me,' I said, once again offering her the ring.
'Oh no, it's a magic ring. It fits whoever owns it,' she said, and with that the ring was on my finger faster than you can fart.
'So, what's it do?' Boglith asked, peering at my finger with open greed in his eyes.
'It has the power to grant its wearer one wish, and one wish only,' she said.

'So what are you going to wish for?' Knobby asked.

'No idea,' I answered.

'I know, you could wish I wasn't a weretortoise,' Knobby said.

With that Geraldine burst into laughter.

'What!' Knobby snapped.

'Sorry, but I've never heard of anyone being cursed with that before.'

'Anyway, that's your wish, ugly,' I said. 'No, you know what I wish? I wish we could just find a tavern and put an end to this nightmare.'

There was a loud noise that can only be described as: Fitzess! and the darkness slowly began to retreat; slowly it moved away until it was nothing more than a memory.

'If you go to the outskirts of town, there you will find a large golden gong. Ring it once and all your wishes will come true,' Geraldine smiled.

'Why?' I asked.

'A Medusa's gaze does not work on women,' she explained, 'so all the women of this village took shelter in a nearby cave. Just ring the gong to bring them home.'

'You mean the small cave just outside of town?' I asked, turning to Knobby.

'Yeah, do you know it?' she asked.

'Oh yes, we wouldn't go in there when it was pissing down, would we Knobby?' I snarled.

Knobby would have replied, but he was too busy being hit around the head with a large stick, which always seemed to appear when it was time to smack someone.

'So, let me get this straight,' Boglith asked, 'when we've rung this gong, what we're left with is a village populated by horny women?'

'Yes. Why, is that a problem?'

'Oh, no problem at all!' Knobby said, running for the gong.

'I'll just go see if he needs a hand,' I said, running after him.

'Me first,' Boglith said, running past me.

'No, me first,' I shouted, shoving him out of the way.

'No, me first!' Knobby screamed.

'Look, me first. It's my wish so I should ring the gong first ... it's only fair.'

'You're right, it's only fair,' Knobby answered, kicking me in the back and running past me.

EPILOGUE

(The bit you might think is the end)

So that's what we did. After releasing the women from the cave, we were hailed as the heroes and saviours of the village. There must have been something about all that free sex and beer because, for some reason, we ended up staying at the village. I moved into the tavern with a couple of very nice girls. Gilbert and his girlfriend got a small house just outside of town, there to raise eggs, or whatever Medusas have. Knobby ended up moving in with a fat barmaid and working behind the bar. In a village of no men, she was the only one who'd take him. As for Boglith, he just took the stool and moved into a small farmhouse, there to await Silmare's arrival. At last we had finally found a tavern that would give us credit, and now all I had to do was remember where it was.